THE STOLEN BRIDE

The Stolen Bride

Illustration: "A South-East View of the City of Boston in North America," by J. Carwitham (active 1720-1740), after an unknown artist. Hand-coloured engraving. Printed for Bowles & Carver, No. 69 St. Paul's Church Yard, London. Courtesy of the Paul Mellon Collection, Yale Center for British Art, Yale University, New Haven, Connecticut.

First Edition.
ISBN-13: 978-0-9863252-9-8
ISBN-10: 0-9863252-9-5

Copy edited by Marcus Trower.

www.adamfletcherseries.com
www.sarawhitford.com

SEAPORT
PUBLISHING

For all of the Charles Jrs. and Annabelles throughout history, who, regardless of their circumstances, had a love and commitment that was unwilling *to be broken.*

THE STOLEN BRIDE

Sara Whitford

Chapter One

ADAM WATCHED HIS MOTHER AS she braced herself on the long table in the tavern kitchen. He could see her knees had gone weak, and she looked like she was about to faint. It was no surprise. After all, she was seeing Santiago—her husband, and Adam's father—for the first time in almost twenty years.

Both Adam and Santiago lunged forward to offer her support so she wouldn't fall.

"Mama," said Adam through a half smile. "Are you alright?"

Mary stared at her long-lost husband. She squinted her eyes and shook her head as if she were trying to wake herself out of a dream. "Are you really...?" She then shifted her eyes to her son. "How did you...?" She turned her head back to Santiago. "I thought you were dead! Adam said you were shot! You were dying!"

Adam could see she desperately needed some explanation, but he also understood she was struggling to find her

7

words. "I thought he was. It seemed hopeless when I left Havana, but thank God he's here now!"

Santiago placed his hand on Adam's shoulder and said, "When I met our son last year for the first time since I left here all those years ago, I felt like I had a reason for living. I prayed more than I've ever prayed before, and I willed myself to heal, to get strong, so I could recover and so I could see the two of you again. I sent Adam a letter once I had recovered and explained that I would be here by the end of September."

Mary looked confused. "I never heard about any letter." As soon as the words left her mouth, her eyes grew big. "Wait a minute…" She looked at Adam. "Is this that letter you picked up in New Bern several months ago?"

Adam nodded. "Yes, ma'am. That's the one—but it was all torn up and damaged, so I couldn't read the whole thing."

"You were so worried about that letter," said Mary.

Santiago smiled. "I heard about that. He was as shocked to see me last night as you are now."

At that moment, Mary threw her arms around her husband's neck and buried her face in his shoulder. Santiago embraced her tightly, and Mary began to sob.

Santiago kissed the top of her head, and with his right hand he stroked her hair to calm her.

She kept her arms around him but leaned back so she could look at him. The pair gazed lovingly at each other, both with tears in their eyes.

Adam simultaneously felt great joy and very awkward. He realized he'd never seen his parents together before, and he'd certainly never seen his mother in a man's embrace—at least not like this. Of course he'd seen Valentine hug her on a couple of occasions when she needed comforting, but that was very different.

He decided he should leave so they could have some time alone.

"Listen," he said. "I've got to get to work now, you two. I'll leave so y'all can visit and get reacquainted. I reckon I'll probably be back here at supper time."

Both of his parents looked at him, smiled, and nodded.

"BACK ALREADY?" EMMANUEL LOOKED SURPRISED to see his grandson coming through the street-side doors of the warehouse so soon after he left for the tavern.

Adam clicked his cheek and shrugged. "Yeah. I reckon those two need some time alone."

His grandfather nodded. "I see." The old man was busy working along a wall of cargo at the north end of the warehouse checking a list he had in his ledger against the casks and crates from the recent plagued shipment. Only a portion of the cargo had been delivered to local merchants because of the hysteria about the "gypsy's curse." Now that that was all settled and everyone would know the real cause of the local sickness, Rogers's Shipping Company could get back to making deliveries.

The large building was otherwise empty. Martin was homesick, and Jones was looking after him. Boaz had the day off, and Elliot and Joe were off in other directions, taking care of different tasks.

Even though the two men were alone, Adam felt like he should cross over to where his grandfather was standing to tell him about what happened with his mother and father. The echo in the warehouse could be awfully loud, and this was a private conversation.

"You need a hand?" asked Adam.

"Eh, I think not—not with this, anyway. I'm only familiarizing myself with what we've got left here—what needs to go out and what I'll be stuck with trying to shift elsewhere. Why don't you pop over and check on Martin? If he was feeling any better this morning, I'm sure Jones will have given him the news about Hardy Green."

"I'll go over and see him in a little while, then," said Adam. Adam and Ricky Jones had just learned the previous night that Hardy Green had died the day before. The man's death would be of particular interest to Martin, since the Casanova had been carrying on a fling with Green's wife, Jenny. "Can I take Rex when I go?" Rex was Emmanuel's horse and Adam's favorite mode of transportation.

"Certainly."

Adam hopped up to sit on one of the crates as he watched his grandfather work. "That was awkward, you know."

"What was?"

He could tell Emmanuel was only half listening.

"My mother and father."

Emmanuel looked up from his ledger and raised his eyebrows. "Oh really? How so?"

Adam shook his head. "I don't know… This'll sound silly I'm sure, but I've never seen them together. It was just so… *weird.*"

His grandfather chuckled. "I see. Well, I can understand how that might take some getting used to." He went back to checking over the list in his ledger.

It annoyed Adam a little bit that his grandfather seemed

unmoved by what he was saying—in fact, the old man appeared amused.

Adam knew he shouldn't be upset. He ought to be thankful his parents were finally reunited, and yet part of him wondered if he might have rushed things by taking his father right down to the tavern like he did. Maybe he should have enjoyed just visiting with him for a couple of days and given his mother fair warning that his father was back in town.

"What do you think will happen?" Adam asked.

Emmanuel strained his eyes and adjusted his glasses. He looked like he was struggling to make out what was written in the ledger. "What do you mean, what do I think will happen?"

"With my parents."

At that, Emmanuel closed the ledger and looked thoughtfully at his grandson. "There's absolutely no way to know. Time can do all sorts of strange things. On one hand, the nostalgia will certainly reignite the embers that once burned between the two of them, but whether or not the flame will last or quickly be extinguished..." He shrugged. "Who knows? Once they realize how much they've both grown accustomed to living alone, there's no telling what they'll do."

Adam wrinkled his brow. "You mean they may not love each other anymore?"

Emmanuel crossed over to where Adam was seated on the crate, and he placed the ledger on top of the higher crate that was beside him and rested himself against it. "No, that's not what I mean at all. But consider your grandmother and I. You met her in Havana, and you already knew me, of course."

Adam nodded.

"The two of us deep down always had love for one another, but if we had had the opportunity to rekindle our own romance after so long, I'm not sure we would have. Too much time had passed, and we had both built our own lives in two different lands. The situation isn't much different with your mother and father. The only difference is they are both still quite young, and when I talked to him before you arrived last night, he mentioned that he's considering moving here."

"Huh." Adam didn't know what to think, much less what to say. "I guess time will tell."

"It always does."

Adam hopped down from the crate. "I guess I'll go check in on Martin." *Anything to change the subject*, he thought. He wished now he hadn't brought up the situation with his parents in the first place.

He asked his grandfather if he should be back at any particular time, to which Emmanuel responded no.

Adam left straight away for Martin's house.

Chapter Two

WHEN ADAM GOT TO MARTIN'S house, Martin was sleeping hard in his own bed, and Jones was napping on the settee.

"Jones," Adam said. "Wake up."

Jones squinted his eyes and rubbed his face to wake himself. "Oh it's you, mate," he said. Adam could tell he was groggy. Maybe hungover.

"How long have you been here?" Adam asked.

"Oh, I stayed right here last night." He patted the settee on which he had been sleeping. "Never made it home, actually."

"What in the world? Why not?"

Jones stretched his arms above his head and yawned, then leaned forward, seemingly a little more awake. "Oh, I popped in last night to check on Mr. Smith just to see how he was faring. Elliott was here and he said Martin seemed to be improving a bit—he weren't seeing no more of them strange visions, anyway. I told him to go on home, and I plopped myself down and fell asleep straightaway."

"I see," said Adam. He looked down at the floor next to

the settee and noticed an empty bottle of Madeira. "Has he been awake at all?"

Jones looked over at Martin, dead to the world in his bed. They'd apparently put Martin's mattress back on the bedstead. "No, at least not that I know of—not since I've been here."

"So, he hasn't heard about Hardy Green yet?"

"Uh-uh. Hasn't heard a thing."

Adam nodded. "Well, you're welcome to head home now if you want. I figure I'll stay around awhile, see if he wakes up. I think I should let him know about the news."

"Sounds good to me, mate." Jones stood from the settee and was about to leave the house when he stopped at the door. "Emmanuel giving everyone the whole day off, then?"

"I reckon. We had an unexpected visitor who arrived while we were gone yesterday."

Jones raised his eyebrows. "Really? Who?"

"You'll never believe it."

"Was it one o' them gypsies?"

Adam made a face at him like he was crazy. "What? No, of course not. My father's here."

Jones nodded. "Oh, that's real nice. You should enjoy a visit with your dad, then."

Adam wondered how long it would take for it to dawn on him what it meant that his father was in town. Not long apparently, because almost as soon as the words had left Jones's mouth, his jaw dropped. "Wait, did you say *your father* is here?"

Jones had been there when Santiago was shot. He knew the terrible condition the man was in, that he was at death's door when they left Havana, so it was a surprise to him just like it would be to everyone that the man had suddenly turned up in Beaufort.

Adam nodded. "Yep. He's here. In fact, I've just taken him down to the tavern so he can see my mama."

Jones looked shocked.

"First time they've seen each other in about twenty years, you know."

"Good Lord! They'll have a lot of time to make up for then, won't they?"

Adam rolled his eyes.

"So why aren't you with them?"

"I'll visit with my father later. I thought they could use some time alone."

Jones nodded. "I reckon they could. Huh… imagine that, after all this time." He looked pensive for a moment, then said, "Well, I'm on my way, then. Send word if anything changes with our friend here."

"Will do."

Once Jones was gone, Adam took stock of the condition of his friend's house. It was a wreck. Everyone had been so busy trying to figure out what was wrong with Martin, and then trying to find him when he disappeared, that no one had time to straighten up the mess after all of the madness of the last few days. The table had been turned back upright, but the blanket was tossed over the top of it. The washtub that had been sitting in the middle of the parlor had been emptied of water, but it was still in the middle of the floor. The furniture that had been piled against the front door, while no longer blocking it, was still not put back in place. Adam decided if he was going to wait around for Martin to wake up, he'd at least help him out by trying to put things back where they belong.

He was relieved to know that the illness that plagued Martin was nothing that he could catch. That made him less apprehensive about handling Martin's things to clean up.

Eventually, Martin began to stir. Adam was happy to see it. He only hoped Martin would be starting to feel normal again. Hopefully, after sleeping off that concoction the gypsy woman had given him, it would be out of his body altogether.

"How you feeling?" Adam asked.

Martin rubbed his eyes and stretched his body across the mattress, then sat up.

"I'm feeling right much better than I was," he said.

"Well, the gypsies are gone now."

"Oh really?" asked Martin. "What happened?"

"It's a long story. I'll tell you all about it, but first I think there's something you should know."

"Fine, but first I need to piss," said Martin. He got up and went outside the back door and relieved himself behind his house. When he came back in, he looked like he felt much better.

"Sounds like you've been sleeping almost nonstop the past couple of days," said Adam.

"I couldn't tell you. I don't remember much."

"You don't remember us having to find you at the top of that tree and bring you back here?" Adam asked.

"What in the world are you talking about?" said Martin.

Adam smiled and nodded. Martin looked skeptical.

"I'll fill you in on all of that later," said Adam.

"Well, if I don't remember, I reckon you could tell me all kinds of nonsense and I wouldn't know any better."

"Why would I do that?"

"Just to be mischievous."

"Yeah, sure. Because I'm always so mischievous, huh?"

"Well, what is it you wanted to tell me so bad?" Martin asked.

"Jones and I were gone most of the day yesterday, and when we got back last night we learned something that I think you ought to know."

"What's that?"

"Martin, Hardy Green is dead."

Martin's jaw dropped. His expression was blank. Adam couldn't tell whether or not he was happy or sad or indifferent. He expressed no emotion whatsoever.

"Martin, did you hear me?"

It took him a second, but Martin nodded slowly. "Yeah, I reckon I did. I just ain't sure if I heard you right."

"You heard me right," said Adam. "He's dead."

Martin looked up. "What happened?"

"Well, the way they tell it, Jenny found him dead on the floor in their house yesterday morning. No one knows for sure what happened, but they're saying it had something to do with his heart—some kind of episode. Who knows?"

"I see." Martin hung his head. "Have you seen Jenny?"

Martin and Jenny were sweethearts from the time they were kids, but when she figured out that Martin wasn't about to settle down, she decided to marry Hardy Green. Martin always carried a torch for her—and in recent months the two began carrying on an affair. Jenny and Hardy hadn't had any children yet. Maybe out of a sense of desperation, Jenny didn't seem to care what direction things took with Martin.

Adam wondered if Martin would take her as his own now that Hardy was gone.

"I don't even know what to make of this," Martin said. "On one hand, I'm sad for Jenny. It's got to be hard burying your husband. But on the other hand, I ain't gon' lie and act like I cared a whole lot about Hardy Green, because I didn't. He was an ass."

"Martin, you ought not speak ill of the dead," said Adam. "And anyway, you only think that because you have feelings for Jenny. Hardy wasn't really such a bad guy."

There was silence between them.

Adam spoke up. "I take that back."

Martin looked up at him with a confused expression.

"I guess I'm tired and I guess I just forgot, but he did want you dead. In fact, I can't help but wonder if his demise wasn't some divine punishment."

"What?"

"Apparently, he went to Madame Endora and paid her to put a curse on you."

"Is that why I was so sick?!" Martin exclaimed.

"No, don't be a fool," Adam replied. "You were just sick because of bad oysters."

"But Hardy Green paid that woman to put a curse on me? You're serious?"

Adam shook his head. "No. I'm not joking."

"How did you find out about this?"

"Remember yesterday I told you Jones and I were gone all day? We had to go after those gypsies. They made off with that barrel with the little girl in it."

"What?!"

"Wait—the story gets even better! The funny part is there was no little girl in that barrel."

Martin shook his head in utter confusion.

Adam explained. "It had been used by Madame Endora's sister to smuggle some things she had planned to sell for profit since the Stamp Act was in effect. She lied and said it was her child so no one would open it. Long story."

"Sounds like I did miss right much."

"Well, you were here convalescing, though I'm sure if you weren't you'd have loved our little adventure yesterday. Boy, you had such an episode with that medicine Madame Endora had sent for you. You were hallucinating and seeing all kinds of strange things. We found you on the edge of town up a tree, and you swore there were rats everywhere on the ground and that they were going to bite you."

"Who found me? You and Jones? Y'all got me and brought me back?"

"No. Me and Elliot and Joe. And as soon as we realized that medicine was making you see things, we poured it out—well, actually we smashed the bottle so the liquid would pour out. I guess it's gotten out of your system now."

"You're tellin a tale!"

"I am not. I'm telling you the truth."

"And Hardy Green is dead?

"Yep. And that's not the only news you've missed while you've been sick."

"What else?"

"When I got back last night, I saw another sloop moored near Emmanuel's at the warehouse. I had no idea who it was—and you'll never guess."

"Of course I won't guess. Who was it?"

"It was my father."

Martin's eyes grew enormous. "Now I know you're tellin tales."

"I'm not. I'm just as serious as I can be. My father was there when I got back to Emmanuel's last night. He was the one who wrote that letter that I've been worrying so much about these last several months. Remember, I only had part of the letter, but once he told me what the rest of it said, it all made sense."

"Well, where is he now?" asked Martin.

"He's down at the Topsail with my mother. I took him down there first thing this morning. It was the first time they'd seen each other in twenty years."

Martin gave a little whistle. "Yes indeed! They sure are going to have some catching up to do!"

It was remarkable how Martin could turn a seemingly innocent comment into something salacious.

"Shut up, Martin. That's my mother and father you're talking about."

"I'm just saying that it's been an awful long time they've not been *alone* together, if you know what I mean. You might not see them for a couple of days."

"Is your mind ever on anything else?" said Adam. "Anyway, it didn't even seem like that. They were just so surprised and happy to see each other again."

"Why aren't you down there with them?"

"Because I thought they needed their privacy."

"Huh. Well, that's understandable."

"Can I fix you something to eat?"

Martin looked like he was thinking for a second. "Yeah, I'd say so, but I don't think I have anything in the house."

"It's alright. I've got Rex, so I don't mind riding to the tavern to get you something—maybe some bread and some soup? Does that sound good?"

"That sounds really good."

"Alright then," said Adam. "I'll be back directly."

AFTER TYING REX UP TO the hitching post outside, Adam approached the door of the tavern. He wondered what his parents were up to. Would they be inside?

His question was answered when he entered the familiar establishment. He saw the two of them sitting at a table by an open window facing the street. There was enough of a crowd that they didn't even notice him come in. The two of them looked deep in conversation. His father's face appeared serious, his brow wrinkled, and his mother's head was tilted the way she did when she was listening with compassion.

It was just as well that they were immersed in discussion, as he didn't intend to go over and interrupt them. He had only come to get food for Martin. He discreetly went over to the counter and spoke to Valentine, who was sitting on his stool behind the bar reading the paper.

"You alright this morning?" Adam asked the sixtysomething proprietor.

Valentine looked up over his spectacles at Adam, then glanced over at his parents, then back down at the paper. "Fine. Doing fine. Had to call in Jackson, since I'm short a server today." He chuckled.

"It's quite a surprise, huh?"

The ruddy-faced old tavern keeper gave a half smile and a nod. "That it is. Coulda knocked me over with a feather when I saw him walk in here this morning."

"You're not still mad at him, are you?" Adam wondered aloud. He figured he might as well ask. After all, Valentine and his late wife, Margaret, had raised Mary since she was a young girl. He didn't approve at all when seventeen-year-old Mary eloped with her Spanish sailor.

Valentine shook his head. "Naw. Don't reckon I have any reason to be mad anymore. Your mama's grown now, anyway."

Adam nodded. "True."

"You not going over to speak to them?" the old man asked.

"Nah. I came to get something for Martin to eat. He's finally starting to feel a little better. Thought I'd take him some soup and maybe some bread."

"Well, go on back in the kitchen. Aunt Franny'll fix you right up."

Adam slipped into the back. Sure enough, Aunt Franny was peeling some potatoes at one of the two big tables in the middle of the kitchen. The old black woman had been working at the Topsail Tavern since even before Mary came to live with Valentine and Margaret. Adam had always known her as "Aunt Franny," but then again, so did nearly everyone.

After they exchanged their usual greetings, Aunt Franny said, "Well, chile, I see you brung your daddy back. Ain't that somethin?"

"I reckon you were surprised to see him this morning, weren't you?"

Franny looked up from peeling potatoes. "I near 'bout thought I was seein a ghost."

Adam laughed. "I bet you did."

"I know you ain't just come back here to visit. What you want, son?"

"My friend Martin, he's been real sick, you know, but he's starting to feel better finally. I told him I'd see if you had any soup or bread I can take him."

Aunt Franny put down her paring knife and potato and wiped her hands on her apron. "Let's see what I have." She went over and looked in the oven.

"I've got some hot rolls gon' be up in just a few minutes—they just need to get a lil' more brown. She looked pensive, then said, "I don't reckon he needs to eat the soup I made this mornin. It's real heavy—vegetables and beef—but I got some chicken stock left over from last night, and I can put that on the fire, throw in some rice, and you can take him that if you think he'll eat it."

"That'll be perfect. I reckon I'll just sit right back here and wait."

"Your mama and daddy's out in the dining room. You ain't gon' go out there and sit with them?"

Adam shook his head. "Nah… I think they're talking, anyway. I'm just gonna let them have their privacy."

The old woman nodded. "I see."

She went to work putting the covered pot of chicken stock, which had sat on the counter near the fire overnight, on one of the hooks over the fire. She went over to the pantry and pulled out a jar and got a cup of rice and poured it into the pot.

In a short time he was on his way back to Martin's house with a jar of soup and a few rolls.

As soon as Martin finished having a bowl of soup and a roll, he surprised Adam by informing him that he was going to see Jenny.

"You can't do that," said Adam. "Not right now, anyway."

"Why not?" said Martin. He stood and started rifling through clothes strewn around his room.

"Well, to start with, Hardy's only been dead since yesterday."

"So? He's dead. She's a widow now. Nothing that says I can't go pay my respects."

Adam rolled his eyes. "Pay your respects? How? By trying to seduce her on her first full day of widowhood?"

"I ain't even got that on my mind at the moment," Martin said, pulling a mostly clean shirt he'd found on the floor near his bureau over his head. "I'm goin to see if I can do anything for her—comfort her."

"Uh-huh." *This is pretty low even for Martin*, Adam thought.

"I'll say this, I ain't gonna let her go again. Maybe God's givin me a second chance to get things right with her."

Adam held his hand to the back of his own neck and shook his head. He knew this was a bad idea—him going to look for her like this—but what could he say to get Martin to reconsider? Probably nothing.

"Martin, listen to me."

Martin looked at Adam with mock attention as he tucked his shirt into his pants. "What?"

"At the very least, you should understand that she's out at the Green farm. His brothers brought her there when they came to get Hardy's body."

"And?"

"And they'll kick your ass if you go over there—rightfully so. It's not like they don't know you and Jenny used to have something between you."

Martin paused for a minute, then collapsed to sit on the edge of his bed, head in hands. When he looked back up at Adam, he said, "How long you reckon she'll be out there?"

Adam shrugged. "I don't know, but if you'll just use good sense and stay put—I mean, just don't go chasing after her yet—I'll keep my ears open and let you know as soon as I hear she's back at the house."

Martin nodded. "Fine."

"Since you seem to be feeling better, you want some help getting this place back in order?"

Martin looked around at the state of his house. It wasn't as bad as it had been when Adam arrived earlier that morning, but it still needed some straightening. "That'd be good. Looks like a hurricane's been through here."

"Huh!" Adam scoffed. "This ain't nothing compared to how it was. You really don't remember much, do you?"

Martin shook his head. "Nope. Just as well, I reckon."

The two spent the next couple of hours cleaning up, and then Adam went back to the warehouse. Martin said he'd head over that way shortly.

ADAM WENT STRAIGHT UP TO the living quarters. Apparently, his grandfather was done doing his inventory of the shipment downstairs.

Emmanuel was seated at the table writing something. He looked up when he saw his grandson come in. "How's Martin?"

Adam came over and took a seat in the chair across the table. "He's doing much better now. He actually had some chicken rice soup and a couple of rolls, so he's awake and his appetite seems good."

"Oh thank God for that."

"What are you doing?"

"Writing a letter. When I finished up downstairs, I stopped in over at the chandlery and visited with Faulkner Baldwin for a bit. We got to talking about the governor's new residence, and he said he had a cousin I might want to send a letter to, to see if Rogers's Shipping can be of any assistance in bringing in materials for the construction and outfitting of the place."

Adam raised his eyebrows in surprise. "Oh really? That would be great!"

"Indeed it would, though it may be a long shot. After all, I suspect it's likely the governor already has men ready to serve him in this capacity, but it never does hurt to inquire."

"Where is the letter going?" Adam asked.

"New Bern. In fact, I was going to ask you to take it into town to see if anyone is going that way in the next few days."

"Why don't I just take it?"

A seemingly confused Emmanuel looked at his grandson. "What? You? What for?"

"We don't have anything pressing to do here right now. I can't see any reason for me not to go. Besides, I like New Bern."

"But your father just arrived last night. You want to leave now?"

Adam took a deep breath. "I'm very happy he's here, but you said yourself he's planning to stay around. I think this might be a good idea to sort of make sure he and mama have time to be alone for a few days."

"Adam Fletcher," Emmanuel said, "if I didn't know

better, I'd say you were trying to avoid being around the two of them."

Adam wrinkled up his nose. "What? I'm not trying to avoid anybody. I just think if I hadn't seen my wife in twenty years, I'd like to have some time alone with her."

"But you're their child. At some point you'll need to spend time with both of them together."

"Sure. Of course. But they can get used to each other again first."

There was plenty Adam wasn't saying, not the least of which was the fact that he didn't want to get his hopes up that they'd get along well after all these years.

Emmanuel was quiet for a moment, then said, "Let me finish writing this letter."

Adam got up and went in the kitchen to pull a pint of small beer, then came to sit back down at the table with his grandfather.

When Emmanuel was done writing, he folded the letter, then sealed it with wax and his company seal, which featured the company's initials, followed by the year it was founded, "RS Co 1723," and he placed it on the table in front of him. He looked up at his grandson and said, "I'll tell you what. You go into town with this today. See if anybody is leaving for New Bern between now and Thursday. If not, I'll let you go Thursday morning."

"Alright." Adam nodded. He stood and took the letter. "I'll be back directly."

"Fine, but don't just go round town and ask men you know won't be traveling anyway just so you can come back and say 'No one is going.' You know what I expect."

"Yes, sir."

At that, Adam turned and left.

Chapter Three

AFTER UNSUCCESSFULLY TRYING TO FIND someone who was going to New Bern by Wednesday, Adam realized he would be delivering the letter himself. He returned to the warehouse and explained the situation to his grandfather. Then he went into his room and decided to write in his journal.

When the episode with the gypsies came to a close, Adam thought it might be a worthwhile story to send in to the *Gazette*. After all, James Davis, the proprietor, had told him the previous winter that he could always use news from Beaufort, so if he had anything interesting, to submit it.

He opened the top drawer of his bureau and took out his leather journal and his pencil and then reclined in his bed and leaned against a bolster against the wall. As he began flipping through the pages to find a blank one, he was now relieved to look at the pages that detailed the bizarre events of the previous week, knowing that all had ended well.

Once he started scribbling everything that he could remember about what had recently transpired, he became enthralled in getting down the details. He flipped back a couple of times to the sketch he had made of Madame Endora. Now he wished he had also made a sketch of Stela, the gypsy woman's beautiful daughter. He decided he'd try to make one—even though he knew those drawings would never end up in the newspaper. It would at least help him hold the memories more vividly in his own mind. He only wished he had the artistic skill of his late friend and crewmate on his grandfather's sloop, Ed Willis. Ed had painted a detailed miniature portrait of Adam in a locket on their way back from Havana the previous year. It was a gift that Adam had purchased in Cuba to give to his mother on his return. It wasn't long after they got back to Beaufort that Ed was murdered at his own kitchen table.

No, Adam's ability to get likenesses down on paper would never be as good as Ed's, but his sketches were at least passable. They were good enough that he'd be able to fill in the details from memory or, perhaps, imagination.

He must've spent hours writing and sketching, because by the time he was done he realized he was straining his eyes to see. His room had been getting darker and darker as the sunlight faded into shadow.

He stood from his bed and reached high above his head to stretch his back. He was about to light his lantern when something outside his open window caught his eye. It was the glow from the windows of his father's sloop, moored just outside the warehouse.

I wonder if he's out there.

Adam decided to go see. He'd only ever been on his father's ship once before—two years earlier, when Santiago had come to deliver a clandestine shipment to Emmanuel and neither of them knew who the other was. He'd helped unload the cargo into the cellar at Laney Martin's house, Emmanuel's "second dock," out at Lennoxville Point. Afterwards, he and his fellow Rogers's Shipping Company workers were invited to visit a makeshift shop on board the vessel to buy trinkets. Adam was broke, but Santiago, detecting the then-seventeen-year-old's curiosity *and* financial circumstances, filled a small cloth sack with candies and Chinese fireworks.

When he made it downstairs to the dock, he felt a surge of excitement knowing he could go right up onto that ship and that it belonged to his father. The man he'd grown up without was now so close, and he was likely to stay around. Adam experienced a moment of heightened optimism that made each step he took feel lighter.

As he boarded the vessel, he saw a couple of the men in his father's crew were sitting on a couple of crates on deck smoking cigars and having drinks.

He was surprised that he remembered some of the Spanish he learned on his Havana trip. "*¿El capitán está aquí?*" It rolled off his tongue easily.

One of the men cocked his head to the side in the direction of the captain's quarters.

Adam crossed the deck and knocked on the door of his father's cabin.

"*Pasa*," his father called out.

Adam opened the door and leaned in a bit.

"*Mijo*, come in." Santiago motioned for his son to enter and sit down.

Adam sat and looked around. His father's quarters didn't appear much different from Carl Phillips's, the captain of his grandfather's ship.

Santiago smiled a sincere smile. Even the corners of his dark brown eyes looked like they were smiling. "This is very nice that you are here and come aboard *La Dama* like this."

"It is pretty nice, isn't it?" Adam grinned, and sort of nodded his head, unsure of what to talk about.

"I just came back from the tavern a little bit ago," his father said. "I thought you might come there this afternoon."

"I did go by there, actually."

Santiago wrinkled his forehead in confusion. "You did? *¿Cuándo?*"

"Probably around noon. I went by to get some food to take to my friend Martin. He's been very sick, but he started feeling better today."

"Your mother and I were in the dining room then. We did not see you."

Adam tipped his head to the side. He felt a little awkward having to explain why he left without saying anything. "I know. I saw y'all sitting over by the window. You looked like you were talking about something important, so I thought I ought to give y'all your privacy. I figured we'd have time to visit more later."

"Ah. *Ya veo.*" Santiago nodded.

"Huh?" Adam didn't know what that meant.

"I see. *Ya veo. Ver.* 'To see.'"

"Oh…" Adam paused for a second. "*Ya veo.*"

His father grinned. "*Muy bien.* Very good."

Adam smiled back and shrugged. "I don't know. Maybe I'll learn Spanish eventually."

"*Sí. Con tiempo, me imagino que aprenderás.*"

Adam made a face the he guessed betrayed his complete ignorance at what his father had just said.

He decided to change the subject. "So what did Mama think about you being back?"

Santiago shifted from side to side in his chair. He looked like he was trying to decide what to say.

"Well, she was surprised, obviously."

"Obviously."

"And I think she was... happy about it."

Adam looked skeptical. "Why do you hesitate?"

"I think she was very—*cómo se dice?*—shocked. There was much she wanted to know. Many questions she had for me. Remember, the last time I saw her was before the invasion of this town—that same summer of the year you were conceived. You saw and learned much in Havana, *mijo*, but she didn't know all of the history, all of what happened. I had much to tell her about, to explain. And she is still very worried."

"Worried? About what?"

"My family. Eduardo."

"But you said Eduardo's dead."

"He is dead, and she has nothing to worry about. I told her that his sons harbor no anger, but she... well... she is not so sure she believes that."

"Hmm. I can understand that. We've had our fair share of duplicitous types around here."

"Duplicitous?"

Apparently that was a word with which Santiago was unfamiliar.

"Deceitful," Adam explained. "Treacherous."

"Ah! *Tipos traicioneros.* Now I understand."

"Anyway, that's probably why she's skeptical when you

tell her there's nothing to worry about. She'd probably rather see that for herself."

"Yes. I think you are right. And I did tell her that I understand, and that is fine."

"She's not mad you're back, right?"

Santiago looked surprised and shook his head. "No, I do not think so. I hope she is not."

"What is she doing now?" Adam asked. He wondered if his mother had sent his father away for some reason. That would be revealing.

"She is working. She said she had already taken the full day away from work, but at this hour, many people are eating, and Señor Valentine needs her help."

"Oh, well that makes sense, then." Adam said it, but he knew better. He knew full well Valentine would've let his mother take the full day off if she wanted to, especially for a reunion with her husband, but the fact that she sent him away meant she needed some time to think. She was either upset or worried or something. Now he was anxious to talk to her and find out what was going on.

It was possible that his father saw through his son's words, because he followed up by saying, "You have to know, *mijo*, that we have not seen each other for twenty years. I was not much older than you, and she was actually younger than you, when we met and fell in love. We have both grown up and grown very accustomed to life alone—not all alone, of course, but without being together. We in many ways are like strangers to each other now."

"I understand the time and what you are saying, but what does it all mean? Are you going back to Havana?"

Santiago shook his head. "No. No, I am not. There is

nothing for me there now. My son is here, and my wife is here. I would like to make this place my home, but of course that does not mean I will always be here in Beaufort. I will have to travel for my work, as I always have. In fact, my crew and I will be leaving next week around this same time for Virginia. I am due to meet some old customers there—merchants in Hampton—by the middle of October."

"How long will you be gone?"

"Not too long. Certainly less than a month. I just have to deliver some things and hopefully line up some future business. Then I will be back again."

"I see."

Adam wished now he hadn't been so eager to take that letter to New Bern. He didn't realize his father would be leaving again so soon. Even though he said he'd be back within a month, he suddenly felt anxious that he might not come back. And now he'd be leaving on Wednesday for New Bern and wouldn't likely be back himself until Friday, which would give him only a few days to visit with his father before he left for Virginia.

"You know, *mijo*, that I had to hire almost a whole new crew to come here. That was not an easy thing to do. My men had been sailing with me for many, many years—most of them before you were even born. It is almost like I am starting over here with *La Dama*, so I will need to find new partners with whom I can do business."

"Why did you have to hire a new crew?" Adam asked.

Santiago chuckled. "If you had a wife and family in one place but your boss told you that you would be leaving home and might not come back for very long, if ever, would you be anxious to go?"

"Oh well, of course not."

"Precisely. I do have a few of my best men from my old crew, but the rest are all new. They are mostly young and do not have families in Havana to worry about. They are happy for the adventure."

Adam nodded. "Well, I reckon they'll have plenty of that, won't they?"

In truth, Adam couldn't relate to the young men who had joined his father's crew. He used to think he wanted a life of adventure, but he'd seen enough of that already to last a lifetime. Anyway, he wouldn't like picking up and moving so far away from Beaufort. He loved his family and his life there too much to want to stay away for too long, but still, he was looking forward to going to New Bern for a couple of days.

He made up his mind he'd make the most of the time he had with his father until Wednesday, but for now he felt like he ought to go see his mother at the tavern.

"WHAT WERE YOU THINKING ADAM!" Mary Fletcher made no effort to hide her displeasure at her son's surprise from early that morning.

Almost as soon as Adam had entered the tavern, his mother had started in on him. He had made it no further than the bar to greet Valentine when Mary made a beeline in his direction from across the dining room.

"What do you mean?" Adam asked, genuinely surprised at her question.

"How unthinking, how *uncaring*, that you would show up at the kitchen this morning—especially after all that's happened around here the last few days—and nearly cause me to drop dead in shock! Couldn't you have at least have come by yourself first and warned me before—?"

"Wait—warned you? Warned you about what? Were you in any danger?" Adam knew she wasn't, but he didn't appreciate her reaction to what he thought was going to be a joyful surprise.

"I haven't seen that man for twenty years, and you bring him by here like he's been gone for just a few months. What were you thinking?!"

"That man? You mean your husband? My father?"

At that, Valentine raised his eyebrows and excused himself from the bar to go wait on patrons.

Mary must've detected Valentine's preference that they not have it out right in the dining room, so she grabbed Adam by the arm of his shirt and pulled him into the kitchen.

Once they were in there, she crossed the floor and turned her back for a moment before she said anything else. Adam noticed her fists were clenched at her side. She was definitely angry. He knew better than to say anything.

"Adam, yes, he's my husband. I said vows to him over twenty years ago *on his ship*, though I doubt the county would recognize it. We had only known each other a short time before then, and we hadn't been married long when he left, and I never thought I'd see him again. You might've well have come in here this morning bringing a ghost."

Adam took a deep breath and sighed. He was genuinely sorry that he'd upset his mother, and yet he still didn't really understand what was so wrong with what he had done.

"Would it have made much of a difference if I *had* come here to warn you that he would be coming by later in the morning?"

"Yes. Yes it most certainly would have! At least then I'd have had a chance to say no or to gather my thoughts, or not be here when he came by, so I could've waited until I was ready to see him."

"Good gracious! Ready for what?"

"Ready to see him, to get my mind prepared to go back there."

"Back there?"

"Back to being a foolish seventeen-year-old girl who got married in a whirlwind and ended up with child before even realizing what she'd got herself into. So I could at least take a few minutes to figure out if I even think I still have it in me to love him and be a wife to him after all this time, or if we'd both be better off if he just went on back to Havana."

Adam couldn't believe what he was hearing.

"When you say 'if we'd both be better off,' who exactly are you referring to? You and him? Or you and me? Because I don't know if you've forgotten this or not, but it took the two of you to make me, and it wasn't the fault of either of you that he had to leave, and it sure as hell wasn't my fault that I had to grow up without a father."

Mary looked at him, speechless.

Adam continued. "I'm happy he's here and I'm happy he's planning to stay, so maybe I can finally get to know him. And to be honest, I think it was a terrible thing that you and Valentine did — always keeping the truth from me about him, making me grow up thinking he'd just left and not come back, never explaining the reason why. Year before last, when I was in Havana, it changed things for me to learn the truth. I was hurt and angry, but mostly I just kept thinking about how grateful I was to finally know who my father was and that he didn't die all those years ago, and that he didn't stay away just because he didn't want to be around, but because he wanted to protect us. You don't think it's been hard on him these last two decades, Mama? At least you had me! Who did he have?"

His mother shook her head and let out a fast sigh and started busying herself with things in the kitchen, a tactic she had used in the past with Adam when he would try to argue with her. He could tell she wasn't happy with what he said or the situation in general.

He decided to try to shift directions. "Anyway, you probably won't even have to see him tomorrow—at least unless he comes into the tavern for a meal. I hope to spend the day with him, because I have to leave on Thursday."

"Where are you going now?" Mary asked.

"New Bern. I need to deliver a letter from Emmanuel to a man there about the new governor's residence."

"And you have to deliver it? Isn't anyone else going that way?"

"Not this week. I've already asked around."

"You know your father's leaving again in a couple of weeks. Says he has to go to Virginia but that he won't be gone long."

This. This is what she was upset about. Adam just realized it.

"I know. He told me. That's why we're spending the day together tomorrow, since I have to leave on Wednesday, and once I get back we'll probably have less than a week to visit with one another before he has to leave on his trip."

"I better get back into the dining room," Mary said. "You know Valentine doesn't much like waiting on folks."

Adam could see she didn't want to talk about any of this anymore.

Adam stood and nodded. "I better go, too, but I'm going to eat something first."

"You go ahead," Mary said. "I'll fix you a plate and bring it out."

Adam enjoyed supper there before returning to the warehouse.

Chapter Four

AFTER SPENDING ALL OF WEDNESDAY with his father, Adam was ready on Thursday morning to head to New Bern so he could be back by Sunday. He had just finished eating a very early breakfast with his father, grandfather, and Boaz—who was as grumpy as usual—when he looked at his pocket watch and shook his head.

"Where is Martin?" he said to no one in particular.

"Hopefully, he's not gotten himself into more trouble," Emmanuel offered.

Adam wondered if perhaps Jenny was back home and he was over there consoling her, though he didn't think he should say anything about it to his grandfather. He asked if he could take Rex to go look for him, when Santiago said, "It just occurs to me... Why bother with that? I can go with you. You will be coming right back from New Bern, yes? It will be a good time for us."

Adam's eyes grew enormous. "Are you being serious?!" He loved that idea.

Emmanuel smiled broadly. "Brilliant! Now I almost wish I could go."

"Why can't you? You're the boss," Adam said, tapping his grandfather playfully on the elbow.

The old man shook his head. "Oh, I'm not much for spending nights at sea anymore with these rickety old bones."

Adam understood. His grandfather had been increasingly bothered with arthritis and in cold weather was often confined to his bed. Even when the days were fair, the nights could be quite cool out on the water.

Santiago stood and said, "I will go down to get a bag of things and will meet you on the dock. I also need to give my men instructions—keep them out of trouble the next couple of days until I get back. This will be a good chance for Beto to look after *La Dama*. He is happy to do things like that."

"Sounds good!" said Adam. "I'll meet you downstairs in a little while."

LESS THAN AN HOUR AFTER they finished breakfast—at about seven o'clock—Adam and Santiago were in Emmanuel's periauger headed for New Bern. Santiago was at the tiller while Adam was tending the sheets for the fore and main sails, as they navigated east on Taylor Creek past Beaufort and into the North River towards the sound. In ideal conditions, they could possibly make it to the colony's capital by midnight, but they were allowing that it might be the next morning before they would arrive.

Since the weather was fair, Santiago predicted they'd make it that night.

As they got farther away from Beaufort, Adam felt a little awkward knowing he'd be traveling alone with his dad for the next couple of days, but he was excited to have the opportunity to get to know him better.

"Tell me about yourself," Adam said.

Santiago wrinkled his eyebrows and chuckled. "That is a very big question. Where would you like me to start?"

Adam shrugged. "At the beginning, I guess. Tell me about when you were growing up. What was it like as a boy in Havana?"

His father tipped his head from side to side and looked like he was trying to think back so he'd know what to say. "I suppose in some ways it was similar to the way it was for you growing up in Beaufort. Are there not some things that are universal for growing boys?"

Adam nodded. "I reckon so."

"But of course in other ways it was very different."

"What stands out to you the most?"

"In the beginning, our cultures are very different. Every day of the week they are different. Havana is a city that is big and busy and old—so there are very many people, and not just *los cubanos*, but people from all over the world, since it is such a big port."

"I can't remember if you told me before, but how did you come to learn English?"

"Ah, *bueno*. My mother taught me English. Her English is not perfect, nor is mine, but she always thought it was important that I learn it. It is a much-used language, of course."

"And how did she learn English?"

"Her father—your great-grandfather—was a government official and a diplomat. He spoke many languages and made sure that his children at least knew *español*, English, and *francés*."

"French?"

"Yes. She never had to use the French much but had to use the English a little more frequently, so when I was small she only taught me English, along with my native tongue."

"So that's how she was able to talk to Emmanuel all those years ago?"

Santiago nodded and smiled. "I suppose so. Yes."

"How old were you when your stepfather died?"

"I was about your age."

"So you grew up with him?"

"Mmm-hmm. *Sí.* He was a very good man, very kind to me and my mother."

"And he was involved with shipping too?"

"He was. He owned many plantations of sugar and tobacco. The estate you saw in Havana was just a small piece of all that he owned."

"And all of that has gone to Eduardo's sons now, hasn't it?"

"All of the Velasquez estate has, yes, but my mother came into their marriage with substantial property of her own. That now belongs to me, and it will eventually belong to you."

Adam raised his eyebrows, not quite sure what to think of that.

Santiago motioned for his son to man the tiller for a moment.

Adam shifted over where his father had been sitting.

Santiago took out something from the small bag he had brought with him. It turned out to be a bundle of food that

Emmanuel had sent for them to eat. He took out a loaf of bread and broke it in two and offered half to Adam.

Adam shook his head. "Not right now, thank you."

Santiago shrugged and wrapped his son's half of the bread back in the cloth and put it in the bag and then he began to eat his own half.

Adam still had his mind on Eduardo's sons. "I know you said your nephews harbor no ill will about the inheritance issues with their father, but what exactly happened with them?"

"It is a very long story," said Santiago, "but to make it much shorter, as soon as I was recovered enough I sent for them. We had a meal together and I told them everything that I knew, with the blessing of my mother, of course."

"Were they mad?"

Santiago shook his head. "No. In fact they were very understanding, and they apologized for how their father had been so determined to stop me from having any heirs to the family's fortune. Nevertheless, I told them that I wanted them to inherit it all—that it rightfully belonged to them. I told them Juan Diego had been a wonderful father to me and given me more than I could have ever hoped for, but that I was happy to let that go for their sake, especially given the fact that they had lost their father."

"I'm relieved to know there is peace among you all. You know Mama is still worried about that, don't you?"

Santiago nodded. "I know. I understand. She went through a terrifying time, and I imagine those memories stay with her. I can see why she would be concerned that, *como la hidra*, as soon as one head is cut off, more will grow in its place."

"I reckon in time she'll see and, Lord willing, be more at ease."

"Yes, Lord willing—as we say, *con la ayuda de Dios.*"

There was a moment of silence between them. Just as Adam was about to ask another question, his father beat him to it.

"Tell me, how are things with you and your young lady?"

"Huh? Which young lady?"

"'Which young lady?'" Santiago mimicked Adam, then laughed. "Are there so many of them? You have to ask which one?"

Adam rolled his eyes and laughed, only slightly embarrassed. "I don't really have a young lady."

"You told me about the one when you were in Havana. Señorita Martin, remember?"

"Laney Martin?"

"Yes. You told me you had your eye on her. Have you made any progress with her?"

"Ha! What a question!" Adam shook his head and rested his elbows on his knees. He looked off in the distance before he answered. It was a little strange having this conversation with his father.

"Does she know you care for her?"

"I think she does, yeah."

"Well, then? What is the problem?"

"You know I still have more than a year on my apprenticeship, right? It isn't like I'm free to get tied up with a girl right now."

"Do you really think your grandfather would stand in the way of you declaring your intentions to this girl? You better do it before someone else does."

Adam's thoughts immediately went to Martin Smith and how he put off declaring his intentions to his childhood sweetheart, Jenny, until it was too late and she had already married Hardy Green. That was different, though. Martin just wanted to keep his options open, and he wasn't ready to settle down. In Adam's case, he wasn't his own man yet and wouldn't be until he turned twenty-one and completed his contract. He didn't doubt his grandfather would be supportive, but still, he wanted to have something to offer Laney before declaring anything to her. Right now he only had good intentions.

"If it's meant to be with her, it'll be, but I don't see the point in getting either of us worked up about having a future together when I'm still so far out from actually being able to do something about it."

"I am telling you, *mijo*, if you do not at least work up the confidence to talk to her, let her know what you want, you may end up regretting it for the rest of your life."

Adam shook his head. "Eh, I don't know. It's not that I lack confidence; I just think it's foolish to start kindling a fire before you have a safe place to let it burn."

Santiago looked like he was contemplating what his son had said. He nodded his head slightly. "I can see the wisdom in that. And while I am not suggesting that you start an ardent romance with this young lady right now, you do her a disservice to not tell her that she has a place in your heart. What if she feels the same way about you but does not think you have a serious interest? Why should she not accept an offer for marriage from another man if she has no reason to think you have it in mind to one day ask for her hand?"

Adam shrugged. "Fair point. I'll think about it, alright?"

His father smiled. "Alright."

"We can stay at her brother's house while we're in New Bern. The Martins aren't home now—they're visiting Will's wife's family in Boston. She just had a baby not long ago. Laney is with them. Will said I am welcome to stay there anytime I am in town while they are away."

"I assume they have someone taking care of their house while they are away."

"I reckon Charles Jr. is. He's a Negro man who's been with Will since he was a little boy."

"Oh, he is a slave?"

"Used to be. They just *gave* him his freedom a few months ago, and he married a free mulatto woman who also worked for their family."

Santiago made a face. "They gave him his freedom?"

"Well, Will gave him the opportunity to work to buy his freedom, but then he turned around and gave the money back to him as a wedding present."

Adam could tell his father thought that was strange. "I see. How old is Charles?"

"I don't know exactly, but if I had to guess, I'd say he's probably around thirty maybe? Something like that."

"Was his *mulata* always free? Or did she belong to the Martins as well?"

"Far as I know, she was born free—or if she wasn't, she had to have been freed as a very young girl. You can tell she has right much white in her. She's real fair-skinned and has light eyes, but she has really curly hair and sort of Negro features."

"I will tell you this: that is one thing that is very different here and Havana."

"What?"

"The slave trade. Back in Havana we have many slave ships every week bringing in Africans. You never see that here, though—not in North Carolina, anyway."

"I think there may be ships that sometimes to go Wilmington, but you're right. I think most of the slaves in this colony came from South Carolina or Virginia. They say it's because we don't have enough deepwater ports for the kinds of ships that bring 'em in."

"It's just as well. It is an ugly business."

Adam nodded. "Yeah. I've heard Emmanuel talk about it. He detests it. Saw it up close back in his pirating days."

Santiago raised his eyebrows. "Oh really?"

"Yeah. You'll have to get him to tell you about it."

As they sailed the rest of the day and into the night, the pair talked almost nonstop. They covered everything from favorite foods, to books, to hobbies, taxes, politics, and anything else they could think of to discuss.

Thanks to continuing mild weather, and winds that seemed to be helping them along, they made it to New Bern around three o'clock in the morning.

Rather than turn up on the Martins' doorstep at that hour, Adam and Santiago slept on the boat until sunrise, then headed into town. Adam was fully prepared to walk the few blocks to the Martins' house, but Santiago reminded him he could hire a coach, which he did.

Soon they were riding down Metcalf Street, and the coach stopped in the circular drive in front of the Martin estate.

Santiago paid the driver, and he and Adam went to the front door and knocked, even though they doubted Charles

Jr. or his wife would be staying in the main house while the Martins were away.

There was no answer.

Adam led his father around the back of the main house to the back garden, where he found Charles Jr. at work feeding the chickens and collecting eggs. Annabelle wasn't around. Adam wasn't sure where she'd be, but it didn't occur to him to ask.

"Morning, Charles Jr.!" Adam called out as he crossed the yard to greet him.

Charles Jr. was a handsome man with a dark-brown complexion and closely cropped hair.

"Mr. Adam!" He put down the basket in which he had been collecting eggs and came over to shake hands with Adam. He looked surprised seeing Santiago, whom he had never met before. "You ain't even got ta' tell me. Y'all's kin-folk, ain't you?"

Adam and Santiago both grinned and nodded.

Santiago extended his hand to Charles Jr. "I am Santiago Velasquez de Leon. Adam is my son."

"You ain't from round here either, are you?"

Santiago smiled and shook his head.

"My father just got to Carolina all the way from Havana—in Cuba," said Adam. "I came here to New Bern just to deliver a letter, and he came with me so we can have time to visit before he takes off for Virginia."

"My word!" Charles Jr. exclaimed. "Y'all's the spittin image of one another." He studied the two of them, then gave a half smile and nodded.

Adam detected something strange about his disposition.

If he didn't know better, he'd think Charles Jr. was nervous about something.

"Tell me, do you know which way Queen Street is? The letter I'm delivering is for a man named Mr. Oliver who lives somewhere along there."

"Oh, that's easy. You jus' go north up this here street. Cross Broad Street and keep on gettin it, then you'll see a street that sort of veers off thataway." He waved his hand in a northeasterly direction.

Adam nodded. "Alright. That makes sense."

"They's a brown house right at that corner, kinda boxy lookin. That there is where Metcalf crosses with Queen Street."

"Good, that helps. We're going to head over that way now. You reckon you'll be here when we get back?"

Charles Jr. gave a deep nod. "I 'spect I will."

As Adam and Santiago started walking out of the garden towards the front of the house, Charles Jr. called out to them. "Mr. Adam, you welcome to use ol' Buck. I can get him hitched up to the wagon."

"No, thank you. We're alright walking. See you in a while."

Chapter Five

IT DIDN'T TAKE ADAM AND his father long to find the residence on Queen Street. Not many people lived on that end of town yet, so the ones who did live there all knew each other.

Once they were done delivering the letter, which had to be handed over to a female servant in the Oliver household, they returned to the Martin estate.

Adam checked the time on his pocket watch. "It's only half past nine."

"I thought we would be done with our business quickly. Now we can make it back by tomorrow. See how the time flew?"

"Mmm-hmm." Adam smiled. "I reckon we ought to go around back and speak to Charles Jr. before we go, at least to let him know that we're leaving."

Santiago nodded in agreement.

They went behind the house to where they had found Charles Jr. working before, but he wasn't there.

"Maybe he's in the main house," said Adam. They went to the back door and knocked, but there was no answer.

Adam led his father to the front of the house just to see if they could spot Charles Jr. there. *No luck.*

"I'd like to at least leave him a note," said Adam. "I suspect I know where a key is. I can go in and write a note and leave it under the door of Charles Jr.'s cabin."

Santiago nodded. "I'll wait here in the front in case he turns up."

Adam went around to the back of the house again to look for a key. He remembered Will saying he kept one in the well. He wasn't sure exactly where it would be, so he closely inspected the inside of the well along the top. Nothing there. He looked up in the little roof.

"Aha!" he exclaimed. He saw a piece of string tucked along one of the short rafters. He reached up and ran his finger along the string to find the end. It led directly to the base joint, where the rafter met the frame. The key was resting there in a narrow space between the frame and the boards that formed the roof. If anyone had seen it, they'd have likely thought it was just a frayed piece of rope that had been blown up with the wind.

He took the key and let himself in through the back door of the house. He went straight to Will's desk in the parlor and found a sheet of paper and took out his pen and ink and began to write a short letter to Charles Jr., but then it dawned on him that he may not be able to read it. He'd never asked if Charles Jr. or Aunt Celie or any of the servants or slaves in the Martin family could read, and he couldn't remember any instances that would've made it obvious one way or another.

Oh well, he thought. *If he can't read it himself, surely he can find somebody to read it to him.*

Adam finished writing the letter and folded it, then was just about to come through the dining room and into the kitchen when he swung the door open and it was caught by Charles Jr.

"Mr. Adam!" Charles Jr. exclaimed. "Whatchu doin in here?"

"My father didn't see you come up? I was just leaving you a note."

Charles Jr. looked down at Adam's hands and wrinkled his brow. "What for?"

"I just didn't want to leave without saying goodbye."

"Y'all's already leavin?"

Adam nodded. "Can you believe it? We followed your directions and found Mr. Oliver's house real easy. Dropped off the letter and now our business is done. It's early enough we can head on back to Beaufort and make it back before lunchtime tomorrow."

"Ain't y'all tired? Y'all don't want to rest here tonight?" Charles Jr. asked. "You know y'all's welcome to stay."

"As much as I'd love to have one of Annabelle's delicious meals, I think we'd best get on back. We really only came to town to deliver that letter, anyway."

"Oh, well Annabelle ain't here. She wouldn't be cookin for y'all."

"Is that right?" said Adam. "Well, I reckon we won't miss much, then. Is she off visiting?"

Charles Jr.'s jaw got tense. He looked across the kitchen to the fireplace, where Adam imagined he'd seen his wife cooking many times. "Sir, I don't have nary an idea where she is, and to tell you the truth I'm right sick about it."

Adam's expression changed. "Do what?" He wrinkled his brow. "What happened?"

Just before Charles Jr. began to speak, Adam held up his hand. "Hang on a second. Let me tell my father we're in here."

Adam went through the house to the foyer and opened the front door and invited his father in. Charles Jr. had followed him as far as the dining room, so Adam suggested they all sit there so he could explain to them what had happened.

They all took seats around the table. Adam sat next to Charles Jr., while Santiago sat across the table.

"Alright, Charles Jr. was just telling me he doesn't know where his wife is," Adam said. He turned his attention back to Charles Jr. "How long has she been gone?"

Without missing a beat, he answered, "'Bout a month now."

Adam's eyes grew large. "That long?"

Charles Jr. nodded.

"Did she just disappear? Did she go to the market one day and not come back?" asked Santiago.

"No, it won't like that!" Charles Jr. exclaimed. "Was this man, he came and brought this letter. Showed it to me and my wife, said while Mr. Will was travelin with his family, we was to let Annabelle go with his wife and children to help them while they get ready to move."

"Did Will write the letter?" Adam asked.

"Yessir." Charles Jr. looked like he was giving the question some thought. "I reckon he did, anyhow, 'cause I recognize his name there at the bottom—with his signature, I mean."

"You read?" Santiago asked.

Adam looked at his father. He was a little embarrassed by the way his father had said that, as if he were asking a horse if he could read.

Charles Jr. looked at both of them and shook his head. "Not really. I can recognize a few words, and I know what Mr. Will's name look like 'cause I seen it so many times, and he wanted me to learn how it look case I need to know for some reason or 'nother, and I can make his name with that pen, but it don't look real good."

"Can Annabelle read?" Adam asked.

"Well, she do read more than me, but she still ain't real good at it."

"Was she able to read the letter? What did it say?"

"She looked at that letter, but I don't reckon she understood much of it. She nodded her head to that man anyhow, 'cause she saw Mr. Will's name too."

"Alright, neither of you were able to read it, but what did the man claim that it said?"

"He said he was the assistant to a man called Harold Singer, and that Mr. Singer work for the General Assembly. Said he was done with his work for the season and was going back home to Chowan County until the next session sets up another meetin. Said the Singers just needed Annabelle to help the missus with the young children while they packed up their house north of town and then was gon' bring her back before they left for Edenton."

Adam turned and looked at his father. He leaned over and whispered to him, "The General Assembly hasn't met for several months, and I heard they won't meet again until the end of October."

"Are you sure this is what the man said?" Santiago asked Charles Jr.

Adam could see the nervous look on Charles Jr.'s face. He didn't want to say anything to further alarm him. "Did he say how long they'd need her help? Or when they'd bring her back home?"

"That man said she'd only be gone a week or two, but after that second week, I kept lookin for her to come home, but she didn't ne'er show up. Then I made up my mind to go lookin for her, and I took ol' Buck out to where they said their farm was north of town, but I couldn't find it. There weren't nothin in that neck of the woods but trees and more trees."

Charles Jr.'s eyes were red and his face was tense. Adam could tell he wanted to cry or scream, but he was using remarkable restraint.

"This man knew that you and Annabelle were free, right?" Adam asked.

"We told him so, on account of how he said Mr. Will was going to lend my wife to him for a time. I mean, she don't belong to him or nobody to lend. She works here with me at the Martins', but they ain't never told either of us we had to go work for somebody else. They've asked us now and again if somebody needed an extra pair of hands, but we could say yes or no. Course Mr. Will's a fair man and ain't never asked us to do nothin outta line, so we always say yes."

"I see," said Adam. He lowered his head and tapped his thumbs on the table in front of him as he thought about what he could say or what he could do for Charles Jr.

"Would you like for us to try to help you find your wife?" Santiago offered.

Adam immediately perked his head up. He was relieved his father was willing to help.

Charles Jr. looked desperate. "I'd sure appreciate it if y'all'd help me out, 'cause I'm 'bout to go out of my mind worryin over her."

"I understand," said Adam. "Right now we can go down to the courthouse and ask around." He thought for a moment. "Wait, have you talked to anybody about this? Asked anybody about this Mr. Singer or his family?"

Charles Jr. shook his head. "Not really. Mr. Adam, for me it ain't like it is for you. I can't just go up and ask folks about my missin wife. Ain't nobody gon' care about some Negro woman, or even a mixed woman, 'less she's somebody's slave and they's some kind of reward."

Adam sighed. He hated to admit it, but he knew what Charles Jr. was saying was, for the most part, true.

"We're going to go down to the courthouse and ask around about this Mr. Singer, see what we can find out," said Adam. "We'll be back as soon as we can."

Charles Jr. nodded and looked at Adam and his father. "Thank y'all. I been prayin every day for her to come back. She ain't come back yet, but when I saw y'all this mornin, I felt like the Lord sent y'all to help me."

Adam and Santiago stood from their chairs. So did Charles Jr.

"I don't know how much help we'll be," said Adam, "but we'll do what we can."

Charles Jr. reached out to shake both of their hands.

Adam and Santiago left the house through the back door, and Charles Jr. followed.

ADAM AND SANTIAGO WENT TO the courthouse first. They went right to the clerk's office. The door was open, but as a courtesy, Adam knocked on the door frame and waited for the man sitting behind his desk to look up and speak to him before coming in.

"Good morning, sir. Sorry to bother you. Do you have a moment?"

The man sitting behind the desk looked like he was probably close to Adam's father's age—around forty maybe—but unlike Santiago, he looked exactly like one would expect someone to look who had been sitting behind a desk his whole life. He stood and introduced himself as Matthew Conway.

Adam and Santiago reached across the desk to shake his hand and introduced themselves.

"Sir, I was wondering if I might inquire about a man who was evidently here in town on some sort of government business about a month ago. I believe his name was Singer— Harold Singer, if I remember correctly."

"Singer… Singer… Now let's see…" Mr. Conway cocked his head and appeared to be scouring his brain for any recollection of someone by that name. "It seems like I remember a complaint lodged by a man with the name Singer, but he's not part of the General Assembly. In fact, if he's who I'm thinking of, it was about a slave who had run away, or had been stolen, or something or other, and they had tried to put an ad down in the paper and came here to lodge some sort of complaint."

"Where does he live?" Adam asked.

"Best I can remember, he lives up in the direction of Edenton. Maybe not quite that far, but he does live somewhere up that way."

"So he came quite a ways here to New Bern?" Adam commented. "Why in the world would he come this far?"

"I don't really know, but I don't think it was actually him who came. I think it was a representative of some sort—a man named Mr. Byrd, I think. He's the one who came on Mr. Singer's behalf. Talked about him like he was a real important fellow. Said he had a big plantation with right many slaves, but he was complaining about, as I said, a slave going missing, and he wanted to make sure it went in the paper. I think he was lobbying for some kind of law or something or other having to do with those who might aid and abet runaways."

"Are there not already laws for that kind of thing?" Santiago said.

"Yes, yes, of course there are," said Mr. Conway, "but these plantation owners, whenever they have a slave go missing, they can act like they're the first person in the world it's happened to and they're outraged about it. I reckon they think if they come to town and raise Cain about it, we'll know they're really serious and can somehow help them get that slave back faster than they might otherwise."

"So if we head up towards Edenton and we start asking around, do you reckon folks will know who this man is?"

"I should expect so. As well-to-do as this Mr. Byrd says the Singers are, seems like anybody up that way ought to know who he is."

"Alright," said Adam. "I sure do appreciate it."

AFTER ADAM AND SANTIAGO LEFT the courthouse, they went right over to the office of the *Gazette* so Adam could talk to James Davis about this Mr. Byrd and the Singers' runaway slave.

Mr. Davis was happy to see Adam and welcomed him with a handshake. He glanced at Santiago, then smiled at Adam. "And who's this fellow with you?"

"Oh, where are my manners?" Adam turned towards his father, then extended his hand in introduction towards Mr. Davis. "Remember that letter I picked up here so many months ago?"

Mr. Davis nodded. "I sure do."

"Well, sir, this is the man who wrote it—my father."

Santiago reached out to shake hands with Mr. Davis. "Santiago Velasquez de Leon, sir. Pleased to make your acquaintance."

The newspaperman smiled and nodded. "Likewise. I shouldn't have even had to ask who he was. Y'all are the spitting image of each other. You're from Cuba?"

Santiago grinned. "Indeed, sir, I am. How could you tell?"

"Your accent. I knew another man from there who came through here a couple years back—you sound just like him. So tell me, what brings you gentlemen by here today? Have you written up some Beaufort news for me, young man?"

Adam hadn't even thought about the piece he had done for the *Gazette* since the night he wrote it. In fact, it dawned on him that he'd left his journal back at the warehouse in Beaufort, so he'd have to get that to Mr. Davis some other way. "As a matter of fact I did write something up for you, but actually we're here on different business today."

"Oh I see. Very well. What brings you here, then?"

"My grandfather sent me here to deliver a letter, but not long after we got here, we learned about a woman who's gone missing. She's a Negro woman named Annabelle... Well, mulatto. She's the wife of Charles Jr. Martin, who used to belong to Will Martin and his family, but he's now a free man and working for the family."

Mr. Davis nodded as he listened.

Adam continued, "Anyhow, his wife disappeared about a month ago. A man came and said that he had a letter from Will Martin that Annabelle was to go with him to help a Mr. Singer and his wife and family get things ready for them to move back home after they've had a term here at the General Assembly."

Mr. Davis's brow was understandably wrinkled in skepticism.

Adam continued. "Well, you know as well as I do that the General Assembly hasn't even been meeting recently, so that right there was a clue to me that something wasn't right. I've asked around, and apparently someone having to do with this Mr. Singer was in town, but he wasn't here for the General Assembly. They say he was here to put an ad in the paper about a runaway slave and then do some sort of campaigning about runaways."

"What was this man's name?" said Mr. Davis.

"I think his name is Mr. Byrd, but the man with the runaway slave—his boss—is a Mr. Harold Singer. I don't know anything about either of these two men other than that this Mr. Byrd was talking mighty big about this Mr. Singer. Says he's got a plantation up around Edenton and has lots of slaves."

"Well, let's see," said Mr. Davis. "Now, you say it was about a month ago when he was in town?"

Mr. Davis pulled the four most recent editions of the

weekly Gazette and placed them on the counter. "Let's look through these and see if we find anything," he said.

The three men each picked up a paper and combed through the advertisements.

"Nope," said Adam.

"Nothing here either," said Mr. Davis.

"Yes," said Santiago. "There are a few ads for missing slaves and missing horses, but none of them mention a Singer or a Byrd or Edenton."

Mr. Davis held up a finger as though he had an idea. "We can go back another month, but if it's not in those, then we're likely out of luck and there was no ad placed by this man."

Mr. Davis pulled four more papers out a long wooden drawer. He handed one to Adam and one to Santiago and he had two himself.

After a couple of moments, Santiago had found something. "Aha! Listen to this." He checked for the date and then said, "This is from the second week of August. 'Five Pounds Reward. Ran away from the subscriber, about the first of August, a Mulatto wench called Peg, about twenty years of age, about five feet, likely, with a bright complexion and blue eyes. She has a scar on her right cheek below her eye and was last seen wearing a straw hat and a light-color calico dress. Whoever brings the said slave to the subscriber in Edenton or procures her so as to be recovered shall receive Five Pounds Reward, and all reasonable charges. Warning, I will bring the full weight of the law upon anyone found harboring or assisting her in any way. Harold Singer.'"

"Huh. Well, there it is," said Mr. Davis.

"Wonder how she got the scar under her eye," said Adam.

"Might be her owner's brand," said Santiago. "If she has run away before, they might have marked her."

"On her face?!" Adam was disgusted at the thought. He'd seen slaves with brand marks on their hands and even forearms, but never one with a brand mark on their face.

"What date did you say that paper was?" Mr. Davis asked Santiago.

"It says Friday, August 13."

"But Charles Jr. said Annabelle's been gone a month, and it's October the second. That would mean this Mr. Byrd came with the letter for Annabelle around the start of September or the end of August. How long in advance do you need an advertisement for it to go in the paper?" Adam asked Mr. Davis.

"The front and back pages are printed at the same time on the same sheet, so we need those notices a few days earlier than the ones on the inside pages."

"That means you would have had to receive this particular item by the end of the first week of August," Santiago observed.

"Ideally, yes. We don't work on the Lord's Day, of course, so we'd either need it by Saturday or Monday at the very latest."

"But this Mr. Byrd wouldn't have had to come to town to place an ad in the paper, would he?" asked Adam. "Mr. Byrd or Mr. Singer could have easily sent the request for the ad placement by post."

Mr. Davis nodded. "Certainly, although we do get folks drop in to hand-deliver a notice like this, being the post can sometimes be unreliable, and of course they might also have other business to attend to in town."

"Let us think about this for a moment," Santiago said, stroking his stubbled chin. "It seems unlikely that this man was in town to place an advertisement, since no advertisement ran after this one in August, so we do not know all of the reasons he was here, but it is possible they do have a slave girl who has run away. It would make sense, then, that they could use Annabelle's help to assist the family with caring for their children and packing."

Adam leaned on the counter and nodded. "That's true, but the thing that worries me is the description of that runaway."

"How so?" said Mr. Davis. "I assure you the scar on the cheek, even if it is a brand, is a small injury compared to some of the runaway notices we get in this office. Some slaves have a terrible limp, the use of only one eye, mangled fingers, all sorts of things. A scar just isn't much of a thing at all."

"That may be," said Adam, "but I was referring to the fact that the description of their runaway slave matches Annabelle. Please read that advertisement again."

Santiago held up the paper and reread the description: "'A Mulatto wench called Peg, about twenty years of age, about five feet, likely, with a bright complexion and blue eyes. She has a scar on her left cheek below her eye and was last seen wearing a straw hat and a light-color calico dress.'"

"Five feet. Mulatto, about twenty, bright complexion, blue eyes. That sounds just like Annabelle," said Adam. "Only differences are Annabelle is a free woman and she has no scars that I've seen."

"Fine. We can go around and around about this," said Santiago, "but someone needs to go and find this Singer plantation and try to learn what has happened."

Adam agreed. After thanking Mr. Davis for his help and bidding him farewell, he and his father wasted no time returning to the Martin estate to tell Charles Jr. what they had learned.

As Adam and his father walked back to the Martin residence, Santiago seemed bothered about something. Finally, he explained what was on his mind.

"*Mijo*, listen. I am very sorry about your Negro friend and what has happened with his wife, but I am afraid we will need to find someone else who can go check on this situation or—"

Adam took a breath and was about to say something when his father made it clear he wasn't done speaking.

"*Or* as soon as we get back to Beaufort, you can talk to your grandfather and see if he will allow you and another one of the men—maybe your friend Martín—to miss working for a few days so you can go to Edenton yourself. You know we cannot go."

Adam was surprised at his father's apparent reluctance to get involved any further. "Wait, why not? You just said back there at the printing office that someone needs to go to this Singer plantation and find out what has happened. Didn't you hear what he said? Do you understand what has happened here?"

Santiago wrinkled up his brow and shook his head at his son. "Yes, of course I heard everything he said, but it does not change the fact that you and I both have jobs to do and we cannot just put everything to the side to go see about this *mulata*."

"This *mulata*, as you say? This *mulata* is a kind, innocent girl who has been kidnapped. The Martins are among my very best friends, and if they knew this had happened, they would do whatever was necessary to help her. Annabelle and Charles Jr. are like family to them."

The tone of their conversation was turning increasingly combative.

"Very good," said Santiago. "Then we go back to Beaufort and you get your friend Martín to go with you. He is part of that family, yes?"

"Yes, of course," said Adam, "but we're already here. It can't take *that* long to get to Edenton. It's so late, it will be tomorrow morning before we got back to Beaufort if we left now, and then it will take probably at least three or four days to sail back up to Edenton, and that's if my grandfather is even willing to let me go again once I get back."

Santiago shrugged. "I am sorry about that, but do you not remember that I told you that I have to have *La Dama* in Hampton in two weeks? I do not have time to go with you now to Edenton."

"I have an idea!" Adam said. "Hear me out please."

Santiago looked at his son with skepticism but gave him a half smile. "*¿Qué es?*"

"You said the mate likes it when he has a chance to look after La Dama. I know he knows how to sail her or he wouldn't be mate. Let's send a messenger to Beaufort for your crew to just meet you in Hampton. Edenton is close to Virginia. In fact, it's probably not even that far from Edenton to Hampton."

His father shook his head. "You are crazy, *mijo*."

"I'm not! I'm serious." Adam was energized. In his mind, he knew this would work. "Listen, Charles Jr. will obviously want to come with us to Edenton to see about Annabelle. Once we've gotten up there and at least found out about this Singer family, you can go on to Hampton if you need to. Charles Jr. and I can stay in Edenton until we're able to get Annabelle back."

Santiago laughed. "And how are you planning to get your grandfather's *bote* back to Beaufort?"

"Charles Jr. and I can handle that. I've done plenty of sailing around with Martin in the sounds and rivers. It'll be a good chance for Charles Jr. to try his hand at sailing. He can even learn a little bit on the way up to Edenton. And Lord willing, we'll be able to take Annabelle back with us."

"Hmm… I just do not think this is such a good idea."

Adam stopped and grabbed his father's arm. "Just think of it this way. It will give us a few extra days to spend with each other, father and son."

"But it will not be just father and son if Charles Jr. is with us." He grinned.

Adam knew his father would likely give in to his argument soon.

"Charles Jr. has his mind on his wife. I just mean it'll be a good chance for us to be away from Beaufort and work and everything. Let's go. I'd rather go with you than Martin, anyway," Adam said. "We've got about twenty years of lost time to make up for, you know."

Santiago reached around and patted his son's back. "Alright, you have convinced me," he said. "We will leave right away for Edenton, but I need to send a letter first to Beto."

WHEN ADAM AND SANTIAGO ARRIVED back at the Martin residence, they met with Charles Jr. in his cottage behind the main house. The one-room cabin was small and sparsely decorated, but it was clean and cozy. Adam could see that Annabelle had put her feminine touch on the place since the last time he had been inside. There was now a rug on the floor and a flowery quilt on the bed. There was also a small pottery vase on the little dining table, but it was presently empty. Adam guessed that when Annabelle was home, she kept it filled with wildflowers and herbs.

The three men sat around the table and Adam and his father explained all they had learned to Charles Jr. He was visibly worried.

"That man ain't said nothin about no runaway slave," he protested. "And he got to understand Annabelle is free—she ain't no slave, and she ain't gon' be for him like no slave."

"Of course she's free, and surely these Singers understand that. You said they had a letter from Will. If Will knows them, they can't really be bad people, can they?" said Adam. He knew what he was saying was nonsense, but he couldn't think of what else he could say to comfort Charles Jr.

"So we gon' go to Edenton, then?" said Charles Jr.

"Yes, and we need to leave right away," said Adam.

"May I use some paper and ink to write a letter?" Santiago asked Charles Jr.

"Mr. Will's got some up in the house. Follow me," he said.

Charles Jr. led Santiago and Adam out of his cottage and into the main house. He then showed them to Will's desk and motioned for Santiago to help himself to whatever he needed there.

"I'm sending a letter to Beaufort with instructions for my crew," Santiago explained to Charles Jr. "Edenton is not very far out of the way if we are traveling to Hampton, and we are due to be there in about two weeks. I am instructing Filiberto, my ship's mate, to prepare everything, and the crew can sail there without me. I will meet them there when they arrive." He turned to tell Adam, "I will also let your grandfather know what is happening here and that we will not be back as soon as we had planned."

"That's good," said Adam. "Make sure to mention for him to tell my mama not to worry. Otherwise, she'll be sick thinking we've both gone off and left her for good."

Santiago snapped his finger, then nodded and said, "Yes, I will do that."

Adam thought it must not have occurred to him to let Mary know where they would be. He suspected it was because his father had been so accustomed to doing as he pleased without reporting his whereabouts to anyone.

"Here I been waitin for Annabelle to come back, but she ain't gon' come back—not on her own. They probably done took her to replace their missing slave and I don't reckon their gon' give her up easy."

"You may be right about that," said Adam. He tried to shift Charles Jr.'s thinking to the matters at hand. "Don't you think you should probably let one of the families nearby know where we're going just so folks won't think this place has been completely abandoned?"

"Fine, I'll do that. I'll be back directly."

Charles Jr. left, and Santiago said he would go to the newspaper office to send the letter to Beaufort with the Friday paper.

Within the hour, all three men were back at the Martin estate, and Charles Jr. had brought along a friend from a couple of blocks over to take the three of them in Buck's horse cart down to the dock where Emmanuel's periauger was moored.

Soon they were sailing away from the town and headed southeast on the Neuse towards the Pamlico Sound. From there, they would sail northward past the Pamlico River and the Outer Banks until they came to the Albemarle Sound, where they would veer northwest, then westward, then north again until they reached Edenton. It would be a long trip by boat, but sailing would still get them there faster than going overland.

Chapter Six

THE THREE MEN SAILED ALL day, spent the first night at the mouth of the Neuse River, sailed all of the next day, and spent that night out in the Pamlico Sound near Hyde County, and then sailed all the next day across the Albemarle Sound, and then—and finally—westward towards Edenton. The town was a welcome beacon to them when they approached the dock late that night. It was too late to go roaming, so they tried to get some sleep in the boat before going into town after sunup.

First thing the next morning, they walked up the town's main street and looked for any open public house or tavern. Adam knew from a lifetime of experience living and working at the Topsail that such a place would be one of the best locations for finding out about local folks.

They found a place called the Old Edenton Inn. There were few places in the colony that were already over a century old, but Edenton was one of them. They went inside.

A woman was behind the bar, wiping down the counter. "Welcome, strangers," she called out. "What can I get you?"

"Yes, sir," said Adam, approaching the bar. "We surely would like to eat whatever you're serving this morning, but we're also hoping you can help us find a man who lives somewhere around here. His last name is Singer—Harold Singer. Do you know him?"

The buxom bar matron tipped her head to the side and narrowed her eyes as she considered Adam's question. She continued wiping down the counter. "Name seems familiar, but I can't place it. What's he like?"

"What's he like?" Adam asked, unsure of what the woman meant. "How do you mean?"

"Young? Old? Rich? Poor? Fat? Slim?"

"I've never met him before, so I can't really answer anything about his appearance, but I've heard he's well-to-do. Supposedly, he has a plantation somewhere near here and right many slaves. He had a girl run away and he'd sent a man by the name of Byrd down to New Bern to put an advertisement in the paper."

"He married?" she said, cocking an eyebrow.

Adam couldn't quite tell if she was asking for herself, or if she was just trying to remember who the man could be.

"I assume so," he said. "They said he had a wife and small children."

The woman tucked the cloth she had been using to wipe the counter into her apron. She turned to speak to a man who was seated a little farther down the bar. "You doing alright? Need anything?"

The man, who was a slender old-timer with an ill-fitting, dusty old red wig and blue eyes and suit a size too large that he'd probably had for more than twenty years, waved his hand a couple of times and said, "No, love. I'm fine. Just fine." He ate another spoonful of his porridge.

"Singer. Singer. Singer. No, I don't reckon I can recall anybody with that name, even though it does sound familiar."

"That's because it sounds like Sanger, my dear lady," interjected the old man in the red wig. "Surely you've met Mr. Harry Sanger. They live just west of town."

Adam, Santiago, and Charles Jr. all looked at each other with piqued curiosity.

"Harry Sanger. Yes, that's probably it," said Adam. "How do we get to his place? How far is it?"

"Ah, well…" The old man stroked his bony chin. "I should think it's about seven or eight miles out to the Sanger place. Just follow the King's Highway north. You'll see a split rail fence along the front of the property and a narrow lane. The house isn't very big, but you'll know it's the right place because of a sign out with their name."

"Do you know where in town we can hire a coach?" Santiago asked.

The overly friendly bar matron smiled. "A Spaniard are you? Lovely accent."

"Thank you, madam," an amused Santiago replied with a smile. "About that coach…"

"See that man over in the corner—the round one?" asked the bar matron. "Talk to him. He has a carriage for hire."

"*Gracías, señora. Estamos muy agradecidos,*" said Santiago, and he tipped his hat.

Adam resisted the urge to roll his eyes. He knew his father was just playing up her interest to his advantage. The woman smiled, and Adam was fairly certain she winked at his father.

Santiago turned his attention to Adam and Charles Jr.

"I will go speak to that gentleman about taking us out to the Sanger place. Perhaps you two get us some breakfast?"

Adam nodded, and he and Charles took a table and ordered food while his father went over and spoke to the rotund fellow with the carriage for hire. Soon Santiago joined them at their table, and within a short time they were being served breakfast—bowls of oatmeal and thick slices of bacon—with a big smile from the bar matron.

Adam was amused at the amount of attention the woman was paying to his father, and he was impressed at how smoothly he handled her friendliness, although he suspected his mother might not have been so amused if she had been there to see it. And thinking of his mother, he couldn't help but feel a little bit proud to know the food at this tavern didn't seem anywhere near as good as what they served back at the Topsail, but then again, they might not've had a cook like Aunt Franny.

After the three men finished their breakfast, they motioned to the carriage driver, who followed them outside, and they began their journey out of town.

Chapter Seven

ADAM SOON LEARNED THE CARRIAGE driver's name was
Mr. Vickers. He looked like he was about fifty or so
and he had unusually black hair for a man his age. It only
had a few sprigs of gray.

His very round face matched his short and stocky phy-
sique. If he'd have come into the Topsail Tavern, Valentine
Hodges would've described Mr. Vickers as a "stumpy" sort of
fellow.

The carriage was pulled by two horses, and when it
started to drizzle a little bit just outside of town, Adam was
grateful that he, his father, and Charles Jr. were protected
from the elements. Mr. Vickers didn't talk much. Every so
often, though, he'd tell them about how much farther it was
until they reached their destination.

Adam always found it interesting how folks all seemed
to have their own mannerisms. Some were predictable and
seemed to fit a type, while others were completely new to
him. In the case of Mr. Vickers, Adam had never met anyone
quite like him before.

He didn't seem unkind, but he wasn't particularly friendly, either. Also, the man seemed like he was very business minded. Adam hadn't had much experience with hiring drivers. Back in Beaufort he usually walked where he needed to go, or if it was quite a distance, he'd take his grandfather's horse, or the horse and cart if necessary. In New Bern, he'd hired coaches, but they only ever took him around town, so the trips were fairly short and there wasn't much time to consider the driver's demeanor.

In this case, however, Adam, Santiago, and Charles Jr. were riding along in Mr. Vickers's coach for nearly two hours when they finally reached the split rail fence and a wooden sign on a post that said SANGER. By the time they reached their destination, it had started raining.

Something about the name Sanger, now that he was seeing it written for the first time, looked ugly to Adam. It made him think of blood, though he didn't know why.

Then his father commented out loud, "I did not realize that name looks almost like *sangre*."

"*Sangre*? What's that?" asked Charles Jr.

Hearing the word spoken out loud, suddenly Adam remembered its meaning. "*Sangre*. That's Spanish for 'blood.'"

It occurred to him that he must've heard the word when he was in Havana and it had somehow stuck with him.

Mr. Vickers turned the carriage right to go down the lane. The house wasn't remarkable. It certainly wasn't a house that would belong to someone with the kind of wealth that the Sangers, or at least Mr. Byrd, claimed they had. On the larger plantations he'd been to, the houses were certainly nicer, and there were usually several smaller buildings detached from the main house for the kitchen, for slave quarters, for storing food, tobacco, and so forth. This residence was no larger than Will Martin's estate was in New Bern, and it really didn't look as nice.

As they approached the house, Adam noticed two slaves working out in a field probably a couple hundred feet away. It surprised him, as it was raining outside, and yet those men were picking the top leaves off of nearly bare tobacco stalks and placing them in a big cart. *Seems kind of late in the season for that*, he thought. Then again, Adam wasn't close friends or family with any tobacco farmers, so what did he know? He could only go by what he'd heard, and he'd heard by the start of October the tobacco was already in the barns and curing.

Between the main house and the field where the men were working was a building that Adam assumed was the curing barn. He saw a white man sitting under a roof that jutted out from the front of the building. He was smoking a pipe.

Mr. Vickers parked the carriage right in front of the house and Santiago paid him. Santiago then asked the man if he'd wait there a little while, since they'd need a ride back into town. Mr. Vickers agreed.

Adam, Santiago, and Charles Jr. debated whether or not the latter should wait in the carriage or come with them to the house to see about Annabelle. Charles Jr. insisted he should be allowed to accompany them to check on his wife so he could see her with his own eyes and make sure she was alright. Adam didn't care either way, but it took some convincing for Santiago to agree. When he finally did, he insisted to Charles Jr. that if he came with them up to the house, he did so as if he were their servant. Charles Jr. nodded in agreement. "That's fine, sir."

As the three left the carriage, Santiago, who was taking the lead, seemed unsure of whether to approach the man under the roof of that barn, or to knock on the front door. Adam decided to take a few steps in the rain towards the barn just to get a better look, but after seeing how the white man out there was dressed, he decided it was unlikely he was the owner of the place. He looked like a laborer, not a landowner. Adam immediately turned back towards the main house and motioned to his father and Charles Jr. that they should go to the front door.

Santiago again took the lead. They went up on the porch and he pulled the rope to ring the house bell.

Voices could be heard inside, though Adam couldn't make out what anyone was saying. Suddenly, he heard what sounded like a man shouting, and finally, a white woman opened the door.

"Good day, madam. Are you the lady of the house?" Santiago asked.

The woman looked flustered, angry even, but nodded. "Yes, I'm Nancy Sanger." She was a surprisingly tall woman of about thirty or so with graying, mousy-brown hair that looked unhealthily thin, and she had a pointed nose.

"I am pleased to make your acquaintance. My name is Santiago Velasquez de Leon, and this is my son, Adam." Adam was relieved his father didn't slip and introduce Charles Jr. That would've immediately created suspicion.

Adam tipped his head. "Pleased to meet you, ma'am."

Charles Jr. stood behind them with his head down, probably in the same way he'd seen so many slaves act in the presence of their masters or other white folks.

She nodded. "What can I do for you gentlemen?"

"We were wondering if, perhaps, your husband might be home," Santiago said.

The woman looked back into the house, then turned and looked again at Santiago and Adam as though she wasn't sure what to say.

Suddenly, a man came to the door. He seemed old to be her husband, definitely over fifty. He was not quite as tall as her, but he was what one might call big-boned, and he looked strong.

"I'm Harold Sanger," he said. "What brings you gentlemen to my farm?"

"Sir, we have just come from New Bern and—"

"You don't sound like you're from New Bern," Mr. Sanger said with an air of skepticism.

"Well, nevertheless that is where we came from just this morning," said Santiago.

Adam was impressed that his father hadn't bothered to explain his accent. It was really none of this man's business, after all, but Adam knew had he been in that situation, he'd have likely said something about it.

Santiago continued. "The reason we are here is we come as representatives of Mr. William Martin, *Esquire*, of New Bern. We understand that you sent a man to town there about a month ago, and he had a letter that you said was from Mr. Martin related to a servant woman who works for him and his wife."

Mr. Sanger wrinkled up his face and said, "I'm afraid you're mistaken. I did send my man, Billy Byrd, to New Bern a month ago, but I don't know anything about a William Martin, Esquire, or any Martins for that matter."

"It seems some folks back in New Bern are confused

about your Mr. Byrd's visit there," said Adam. "A couple of men we talked to were under the impression that you serve in the General Assembly and that you required the temporary assistance of a servant woman to help your wife and small children with the move back here after spending a time down in Craven County."

Adam stopped talking for a moment and listened.

"I hear small children in your house, so I would assume it's at least true that they are yours, though I'm not sure about the rest of what we'd heard."

Mr. Sanger let out a loud laugh. "Me! The General Assembly! What kind of nonsense is that? I'm sorry to say it, but it sounds like you've come a long way on a fool's errand."

"Well, sir," Santiago said, "we have also heard another story that your man Byrd was there because you had a slave that had run away and there was some concern about that. He had intended to place an advertisement in the paper when he was there in town."

"Now that part is true," said Mr. Sanger. "I did have a wench run away, but she's back now. Good ol' Billy was able to track her down and bring her back here. Isn't that right, Nancy?" Harold turned his head and called back into the house and waited until he heard his wife respond "That's right, Harold" before returning his attention to the men on his front porch.

"Where did Mr. Byrd find the woman?" Adam asked.

"Down there in Craven County I reckon," said Mr. Sanger.

Adam quickly stole a glance at Charles Jr. He could see that the man was feeling anxious, but he was hiding it well.

"Sir," Santiago said, "this situation is a bit irregular to be sure, but it so happens that around the same time your Mr. Byrd *found* your mulatto woman, a mulatto servant woman was taken from the estate of our Mr. Martin, and she has not been returned. It was evidently by a letter presented by Mr. Byrd to this mulatto woman's husband, Charles Jr., that his wife, Annabelle, was enticed away from her station at the Martin estate."

"What are you getting at?" asked Mr. Sanger.

Adam was getting impatient. "Sir, may we meet your mulatto woman? It would put our minds at rest if we could see her and know that she is not Annabelle Martin."

"Ho ho! Do you think I was born yesterday?" Mr. Sanger guffawed. "I know what this is: you two scoundrels are trying to concoct some ridiculous tale to steal away one of my slaves. Well, let me tell you what, you damned well better think again. I'll bury the two of you right here in my yard if you even try!" He pushed his way past Adam and his father and walked to the corner of his porch, where he could call out into the field where the slaves were working. "Billy! Come on over here!" he bellowed.

Adam, Charles Jr., and Santiago exchanged concerned glances.

"Mr. Sanger," said Santiago, "I can assure you we have come here to do no such thing. We are only trying to learn what may have happened to Mr. Martin's servant woman, and we have followed the clues we have been given thus far and they have led us to your front door. That is all. We only ask if we might see your mulatto woman. If she is not Annabelle, we will leave immediately and you will never hear from us again."

The man called Billy Byrd came up onto the porch and

completely ignored Charles Jr., but he looked Adam and Santiago up and down before asking Mr. Sanger, "Yes, sir, what can I do for you?"

Mr. Sanger held up a finger at Mr. Byrd as if to say, *Wait a minute.* He then looked sternly at Santiago and Adam and said, "And what if you meet this woman and then lie and claim she is your mulatto?"

"Impossible, sir," said Santiago. "In the first place, Annabelle Martin is a free woman. She has been free her whole life, so she is not *our* mulatto. In the second place, we both fear God so we do not lie. If we meet this woman and we believe that she is Annabelle, we will tell you so and then we will go back into town and consult with counsel on how we should resolve the issue. We do not have interest in conducting ourselves in a way that is outside of the law."

It took every bit of patience Adam had not to roll his eyes at his father's speech. He actually wanted to beat the living daylights out of this man, who was clearly trying to intimidate him and his father. He never did have much patience for bullies.

"Billy, go on to the back porch and fetch Peg and bring her here."

Billy Byrd wrinkled up his forehead and shook his head. "I don't know that that's such a good idea," he said.

"You hush and go on and do what I told you," demanded Mr. Sanger. He went to grab at Byrd's shoulder and nearly missed. Adam made a mental note of that.

Billy shrugged and stepped down from the porch and went around the house. Within a minute or two, he returned around the side of the house with a light-skinned woman.

She had a scarf wrapped around her head and she hung her head down.

Adam watched Charles Jr. and wondered how he'd react if it was Annabelle. And if it was her, how would *she* react?

This whole situation felt uncomfortably precarious.

"Step on up here, Peg," said Mr. Sanger. "These men want to get a good look at you."

Peg reluctantly stepped up on to the porch and slowly lifted her head. At no point did Billy Byrd let go of her upper arm, which he gripped tightly in his leathery hand.

Adam stepped forward and looked at her. He couldn't see her hair, but he could see that she had swelling and a bruise across the right side of her face and eye. It also appeared that she had a scar across that same cheek, but while the swelling and bruise looked like the result of an angry backhand, the scar on her cheek looked like it had been made with a knife.

In spite of all of that, Adam knew that this was obviously Annabelle. He gave a quick, tense look at Charles Jr., then at his father. He prayed no one would react rashly.

For a brief moment, Charles Jr. looked up and saw it was his wife. He gasped, just slightly. Adam hoped Mr. Sanger hadn't noticed.

When Adam's glance met with Annabelle's, even though one of her eyes was swollen almost shut, the other eye grew large, though she immediately tried to hide her surprise.

"Annabelle," said Adam, "it *is* you. We've come to bring you home."

The pitiful young woman looked terrified. Adam felt anger burning in his chest, wondering what she had gone through these last many weeks. He could only imagine the rage and concern that Charles Jr. felt. He marveled at his restraint.

Although Santiago had never met Annabelle, he didn't hesitate to confirm her identity. "This is Annabelle Martin," he said matter-of-factly. "We will need to take her back with us to New Bern post haste, but do not worry. We will go into town first and—"

"You're a damned liar!" Billy Byrd interrupted. He squeezed her arm and pushed her forward. "This is Peg. Just Peg. She's a slave and she has no other name."

"Calm yourself, Billy," said Mr. Sanger. "I've already figured out what these two are up to. They're trying to steal my property, but I've already warned them if they don't carry their thieving selves away from here, I'll bury them myself."

Adam stepped forward, but his father put his arm out to hold him back.

"I already told you, there is no need for violence, Mr. Sanger," said Santiago. "This *is* Annabelle Martin. That means *your* slave woman is still at large and you have wrongly taken possession of a free woman. Now, my son and I and our servant here are going to get into that carriage and go back into town and talk to an attorney to find out the proper course of action for us to take here. But let me warn you about one thing—you do not know us, and you do not know the power we are capable of bringing here with us. If we return to this farm and we discover you have done something with Annabelle, we will bring Hell itself down upon this place, and *we* will bury *you* on your own little farm. Make no mistake about it."

As they walked back towards the carriage, Sanger shouted

at them. "Like hell you will! I'm not blind! I'm not blind! You're not gon' take my slave!"

As soon as Adam, Charles Jr., and Santiago had climbed back into Mr. Vickers's carriage and were on their way down the lane back to town, Charles Jr. said, "Y'all got to let me out. I gotta go get my wife!"

Adam looked worriedly at his father. This was going to be a difficult situation.

"You do not want to go back there just yet," Santiago said, shaking his head.

"They've struck her. Didn't y'all see that bruise on her face?" He reached for the door handle, but Santiago moved Charles Jr.'s hand away.

Charles Jr. had a look of rage combined with fear that unsettled Adam. He imagined that it was taking every bit of self-restraint Charles Jr. had to not push his way out of the carriage and run back to beat the living daylights out of Sanger and Byrd, and he wondered what Charles Jr. might do if he was prevented from going.

Santiago shook his head, then called out for Mr. Vickers to step up the pace a bit.

"Please! I'm begging you!" Charles Jr. winced through gritted teeth. "Please just stop this carriage and let me out, else I'm gon' jump!"

He sounded desperate. Adam didn't doubt he'd try.

Santiago put his hand in front of the door and held his other one up to motion for Charles Jr. to stop persisting. "You will not do anything of the sort. You know that if you step one toe out of line there will be no mercy for you from these people. We do not know what their attitudes are towards slaves or free Negroes—so you will just have to be patient and wait for us to make some progress here through the legal channels."

Charles Jr. pressed his back hard into the seat behind him and turned his head to look out the window at the Sanger farm, which was drifting far into the distance.

"Listen," said Adam. "We're going to get Annabelle back, but we have to try to handle this the right way, or it will cause both of you a lot more problems that you might realize. Lord willing it won't come to this, but we might even have to get Will Martin down here to sort all this out. So, as hard as it is, you're just going to have to be patient and trust us. Besides, I know if we fail at helping you with this, we won't only be facing the wrath of your mama but Miss Laney will rake me over hot coals."

Santiago chimed in, "I suspect they will be cautious about their treatment of your wife now that they know we are getting the authorities involved."

"Did y'all notice the way Harold Sanger missed when he tried to grab Byrd by the arm?" Adam said. "I'm wondering if his eyesight is bad and Byrd has taken Annabelle because she might look enough like Peg to fool Mr. Sanger. Maybe if we press this matter hard enough, Mr. Sanger will realize his own overseer is trying to deceive him and he'll willingly give Annabelle back."

Charles Jr. did not look convinced. He said nothing, but Adam could tell he was biting so hard on the inside of his cheek that it would be a miracle if it wasn't bleeding. He looked like he wanted to cry, but Adam knew Charles Jr. would never let anyone see him do that—if he ever even shed a tear at all.

Chapter Eight

THE TRIP BACK TO THE tavern in Edenton felt like it took a lot longer than the trip out to the Sanger place. The three men were all anxious to find legal help so they could rescue Annabelle, and Charles Jr.'s fear, though completely understandable, was palpable. The sooner they could find a lawyer, the better.

When they first rolled into town, Santiago called out for Mr. Vickers to pull the carriage over for a moment. The roly-poly driver did as he was asked, and Santiago climbed out to speak to him.

"What if they ain't no lawyers around here like Mr. Will?" Charles Jr. said to Adam.

Adam understood what he meant. Will and his family treated black folks with a kindness and dignity that was unusual in most quarters. While there were attorneys who were sympathetic to the unique challenges faced by free people of color, others were primarily concerned with keeping their deep-pocketed, plantation-owning, slave-holding clientele happy, and they had little interest in advocating for Negroes.

Nevertheless, Adam was sure they'd find a sympathetic ear. There were kind folks everywhere, and though they might have been at times challenging to find, they were around.

Soon Santiago climbed back in and nodded. "I think he knows of exactly the right man who will help us. He will take us there now."

"I hope you're right," said Adam.

ADAM, HIS FATHER, AND CHARLES Jr. sat in front of the large mahogany desk in Walter King's law office while they waited for him to finish seeing off another client—an older woman whose husband had recently died. Adam had overheard she was being sued by the man's surviving children over a dispute related to his estate—apparently, about money from the sale of some of his slaves.

If Charles Jr. was uneasy with this lawyer handling this sort of case, he wasn't showing it. Adam knew, however, that it was likely that Will Martin had handled similar cases back in New Bern, so Charles Jr. understood that was part of the profession.

Soon Mr. King returned to his office from the foyer, and he took a seat in the large chair behind his desk. This man's office was the fanciest Adam had ever seen, but then he'd heard there was a lot of old money up in Edenton, so he wasn't too surprised.

"Sorry to have kept you waiting," Mr. King said. "You say you may require my services."

Santiago nodded. "Yes, sir. Thank you for taking the time to see us on short notice. My name is Santiago Velasquez de Leon, and this is my son, Adam." He motioned to him. "And this other fellow here with us is Charles, a free Negro who works for a friend of our family, Will Martin, Esquire, in New Bern. Mr. Martin has traveled to New England with his family for the next few months, and he left Charles Jr. and his wife, Annabelle, here to look after their place while they are away. However, several weeks ago a man from nearby—a Mr. Byrd—came to New Bern claiming to represent Mr. Martin and under false pretenses enticed Annabelle to leave with him based on the understanding that she was going to offer help for a short time to the wife of a legislator. They disappeared with Annabelle, and now we have located her on a local farm, about seven miles from here, and we would like your assistance to secure her freedom from the man who is holding her as a slave."

Mr. King sat back in his chair and said, "My, my, that's quite a story, Mr...?"

"Velasquez. You may just call me Mr. Velasquez if you please."

"Mr. Velasquez, hmm... Well, I'm afraid we find ourselves in a difficult position. I don't know you, and you don't know me, and yet you've just explained to me that you're here representing a lawyer friend from New Bern, who isn't even in the colony right now, and that you want me to go help you recover a free Negress who's being held here against her will. Surely you understand I'm going to need a little more proof that you are who you say you are and that you represent who you claim. Do you have any contacts here in Edenton who know you?"

"I am a shipping merchant and I have conducted business with clients all up and down this coast. There was a man here many years ago named Mr. Matthias Blount who used to know me, but I heard he died last winter. I can assure you, however, that my money is good, and if necessary I am happy to travel out to his plantation north of town to see if his wife or sons are there, because they will surely remember me."

"Well, well, well," said Mr. King. "It just so happens that Providence is looking favorably upon us today, because his youngest son, Pearson Blount, is my apprentice. He's out on an errand for me and should be back directly."

"I know Pearson," said Santiago. "He will know me."

"Good. Once he's confirmed what you say, we'll be able to take some action, but in the meantime, perhaps you can explain a bit more to me about your predicament."

Santiago and Adam proceeded to tell Mr. King everything that had happened. Charles Jr. was asked a few questions, and he answered them. Mr. King wasn't particularly friendly to Charles Jr. Adam could tell this was likely the man's first case helping anyone who wasn't white, but he was nevertheless professional.

When the three were done explaining everything, Mr. King took a deep breath, and then he sighed. He leaned forward in his chair and rested his elbows on his desk, crossing his hands in front of him.

"I'm going to just tell you exactly how it is. My only experience with Negroes is handling slave-owner disputes— usually when some slave has run off and is being sheltered by some other man or woman. I'll go 'round and take a letter and explain that I'm representing whoever the slave owner is and I've come to take the slave back to its rightful owner, and, if they don't surrender the slave, that I'll take them to court and sue them for everything they've got."

"So you cannot—or you will not—help us, then," said Santiago.

"I didn't say that," said Mr. King. "I just wanted to tell you that because it perhaps makes what I'm going to say next all the more remarkable. I know Harold Sanger and I know that fool overseer of his, Billy Byrd, and they are an embarrassment to all of Chowan County. Harold Sanger would've never been able to acquire that little spit of dirt if it weren't for the fact that his wife inherited it. And if you've seen her, you know the land's what made him take the vows."

He lowered his eyes and gave a grin like he thought his comment was funny. When Adam and the others failed to respond with amusement, Mr. King cleared his throat and continued. "That man never owned a slave in his life until he married that pitiful woman and moved into that house. Ever since he moved out there, he's been uppity. You can always tell new money, because that there is exactly how they act. I represent clients who've been in this colony for nearly a century and they have fine plantations and plenty of slaves, but I ain't never seen any real gentleman behave like that horse's ass."

Adam wasn't sure what the purpose was of Mr. King's speech, but he hoped he'd soon get to it. He could see that Charles Jr. was not at all impressed with their potential representative.

Apparently, Santiago was thinking the same as Adam, because he said, "Mr. King, are you going to help us or not?"

"I'll be glad to. In fact, I'm not even worried whether or not Pearson Blount can attest to who you say you are. Just knowing that Harold Sanger and Billy Byrd are involved with this, I have no doubt that what you say is true, because I know their characters. This all sounds exactly like something they would do. They don't really associate with anyone in town. I think Sanger knows folks don't think well of him around here. That said, this gives me an excuse to satisfy my own curiosity to go and see exactly what kind of place he's running out there."

"What will you be able to do?" Adam asked. "Can we go and take Annabelle?"

"We present the facts to Mr. Sanger—that he's wrongfully detaining a free woman—and we'll insist he turn her over to us, but it's anybody's guess whether he'll do it or not. If he decides to be stubborn, we may end up needing Mr. Martin, as her regular employer, to come and intervene. Then we could get the constable involved, but let's hope we can resolve things ourselves. Otherwise, the girl might be forced to stay out there until whenever Mr. Martin comes back down south."

When they were all done talking, Adam and his father had a word in private and they decided it didn't make much sense for all of them to ride back out to the Sanger place, especially with Charles Jr. in the state he was in. Adam agreed to take Charles Jr. back to the tavern and to try to get a room there, or somewhere nearby, and they'd wait until Santiago and Mr. King returned before deciding what to do next.

BACK AT THE OLD EDENTON Inn, Adam had a brief conversation with the bar matron, whom he learned was called Hetty—short for Henrietta—and of course she asked if "that Spaniard" would be staying as well.

Adam said that he thought so, but he wouldn't know for sure until he returned—or not.

He and Charles Jr. went upstairs to their room to rest for a bit while Santiago was gone. Sleeping while sailing came easily for some men, but it was always something that took some getting used to for Adam. Since he didn't make overnight sailing trips often, he hadn't gotten much sleep on the trip from New Bern to Edenton, or the trip from Beaufort to New Bern before that.

Charles Jr. never made overnight sailing trips, but it seemed apparent to Adam that Charles Jr. couldn't rest right now if his life depended on it. His mind was fixed on Annabelle.

"We'll get her back," said Adam. "We will."

Charles Jr. reclined on his cot but stared straight ahead.

"Think of it this way," Adam said. "We found her. Imagine how we'd feel right now if we'd come here to Edenton and no one had ever heard of Singers or Sangers or whatever."

Charles Jr.'s head dropped. He sighed. "You're right, but now I know they've struck her. Ain't no tellin what those men done to her. You know what those kind of men can do to Negro women?"

"I do know what some do, but don't think Negro women are the only ones who are abused in that way."

Charles Jr. stood from the cot and walked over to the window and looked out.

"Try not to let your thoughts run wild," Adam said. "You don't have any reason to think right now that they have done anything like that to her."

"I don't have any comfort that they haven't."

"Maybe you don't have any assurance that they haven't, Charles Jr. Lord willing, that mark on her cheek is the only abuse she's suffered—other than being kidnapped, of course."

"I know what my mama would say," Charles Jr. said. He

let out a little "Heh!" Then he nodded. "Yeah, I know exactly what she'd say."

"What's that?"

"She'd say, 'I told you so, you stubborn child! Whatchu want that freedom for, anyway? You ain't really gon' be free if you a Negro. Whatchu want to leave the care and protection of the Martins for?'"

Adam narrowed his eyes and wrinkled his brow. "I don't think she'd say that right now. She'd know you're worried sick, and she'd be worrying right along with you for Annabelle. She'd probably just tell you to get on your knees and pray, and that no matter what, everything would be alright."

"You don't know my mama. You don't know what she'd say!"

"Granted, I don't know her as well as you do, but have you forgotten that we were just talking about you buying your freedom about a year ago? I know how she worried over it, but I also know that when you did marry Annabelle, she was as proud as she could be. She's your mama. She loves you. She wants the best for you and Annabelle. Remember, she's got her mind on grandchildren. How are you going to give her grandchildren if we don't rescue your wife?"

"Maybe this whole mess is the Lord's way of showin me I shoulda listened to my mama, and that I was a fool if I thought I was gon' really be a free man with a free wife and a free family."

"That's a terrible thing to say, and you should know better," said Adam. "Do you really think you should have stayed a slave when Will Martin was willing to emancipate you? Would the Lord have been more pleased with you if you had done that after He clearly gave you a path to freedom? If you think that, how can you explain the Exodus? Was God pleased with the Hebrews, who constantly complained, worrying about following Moses out of their bondage in Egypt when here He was, using Moses to guide them to freedom? Of course not."

Charles Jr. dropped his head. He didn't respond. Adam wasn't sure whether his friend understood what he was trying to say and agreed, or he was mad about it and didn't want to talk anymore. He decided it might be easier on both of them if he just bowed out of the conversation and got some sleep. Maybe Charles Jr. would take the opportunity and rest as well.

Chapter Nine

ADAM HAD SLEPT HARD FOR what must've been a couple of hours when he was awakened by a knock at the door.

Charles Jr. went over to answer it. It was Santiago.

"What did you find out?" Charles Jr. asked.

Santiago took a seat at the foot of Adam's bed. Charles Jr. sat in the chair next to the window. Adam figured he must feel like he shouldn't sit on the only other bed, since it would likely be Santiago's to sleep in that night.

"Harold Sanger now understands he is in some trouble. Mr. King made an impressive case for all of the ways in which Sanger and Byrd are violating laws, and he made it clear that we will not hesitate to bring every available action against them to achieve our desired ends. Also, Mr. King advised we take his friend, Dr. Bass, out there as another witness because of her injuries, so we did. We requested that Mr. Sanger allow Dr. Bass to examine Annabelle, and surprisingly, he did at least allow him to look at her on the porch, but he did not allow Dr. Bass to treat the mark on her face."

Charles Jr. looked confused. He shook his head. "When do we get my wife back?"

Santiago sighed. He clasped his hands together and dropped them into his lap. "We have to get Will Martin here to speak for both of you."

"What!? Why?" Charles Jr.'s eyes betrayed his panic.

"You were only just emancipated a few months ago, and you are still his employee. Charles, you understand that a judge is not going to listen to the testimony of a black man against a white man, even if he is a detestable white man. We need Will Martin to come here to not only assist us in securing Annabelle's freedom but also in bringing charges against Sanger and Byrd for fraudulently claiming to represent him and lying about Will writing that letter."

Adam looked at Charles Jr., who didn't seem even remotely consoled by what he'd just heard Santiago say.

"This is a good thing. Do you understand?" Adam asked him.

Charles Jr. looked down at the floor and said something unintelligible.

"What?" said Adam.

Charles Jr. looked up at him. "I know I might never get my wife back this way. It'll take a month or more for Mr. Will to even find out that we need his help. It's a lot colder up there than it is here. There might even be snow. Ain't no tellin how long it'll take him to get back down here, or if he'll even be in a hurry to come. He's up there with his wife and that new baby and Miss Laney and all, and he won't plannin to come back till after Christmas."

Santiago looked at Adam and shook his head. Adam could tell his father's patience was wearing thin. He didn't have experience with any of these people in the Martin family well enough to know what to say to Charles Jr. in this situation.

Adam said, "Charles Jr., we're going to Boston. We're going to find Will and bring him back. I have no doubt he'll be just as anxious as we all are to resolve this. Don't forget, Sanger and Byrd have done something evil by using his name, *and* they've kidnapped a woman who is not only in his employ but someone who—and I have little doubt of this—he considers a part of his extended family, just as he considers you and Aunt Celie."

"I don't want to leave here," Charles Jr. countered. "I need to stay close by and make sure my wife is alright."

"You can't be running out to the Sanger place every day to check on her," said Adam. "I don't think he or Billy Byrd will allow that, and they're liable to—"

"Wait, son," Santiago interrupted. "I think Charles is right. He should stay close by for his wife. He may not be able to see her every day, but I think we can let Mr. King know that he will be staying here in town, and perhaps he can go with him on some days to check on Annabelle, even if they do not confess who he is. He can pose as our servant, just as he did earlier today, and they will have a visible reminder that we have gone to bring back the man who will make them pay for what they have done—and it will only be worse for them if they make another misstep."

"Do you trust Mr. King enough to handle that the way you are suggesting?" Adam said. "Do you think he'll be alright with Charles Jr.?"

"He is perhaps not as considerate as someone like your friend Will Martin, but I think he is trustworthy, and I think that he will do what we ask him to do. After all, we are paying his bill, are we not?"

Charles Jr.'s expression changed to one that almost

looked hopeful. He spoke to Adam, "I'm real grateful for all y'all are doin and all y'all done so far. And I think it's real good of you to be concerned for me and Annabelle, but don't worry 'bout me. I can take care of myself alright. Mr. Will's a good man, but there's been times I've gone to help other folks at Mr. Will's request and they've not been so kind. I know how folks can be, and I know how to do what I got to do to get along. I ain't gon' do nothin to hurt my chances of gettin my Annabelle back."

Chapter Ten

WHEN ADAM, SANTIAGO, AND CHARLES Jr. were done talking and all had been decided about their strategy going forward, Adam said he was hungry. Santiago was, too, but Charles Jr. wanted to stay in the room and rest. He said he needed to get some sleep. Adam was glad he finally seemed relaxed enough to do that.

He and his father went downstairs to eat in the tavern dining room and to discuss their plans for leaving the next morning.

Since Adam hadn't traveled to Boston before, he had no idea what their trip would involve.

"First thing in the morning, we will go with Charles to Mr. King's residence, because I doubt he will be in his office yet," his father explained. "He told me where he lives and said it would be fine to come by early. I am going to give him a payment to retain his services and to provide food and lodging for Charles Jr. Then we need to either hire a coach or find some other means of traveling by road to Virginia."

Just then a young barmaid came to ask them what they

wanted to eat. She was close to Adam's age and unlike the flirty older woman who'd served them previously, this girl kept her eyes down as she took their order. She explained there were only two choices—fish stew or chicken.

Adam asked for the chicken. Santiago wanted the fish stew. Small beer would come with the meal, but Santiago ordered some rum as well. The young woman disappeared into the kitchen, and Adam and his father continued their conversation.

"How long should that take us?" Adam asked.

"We will be taking the Virginia road to Constant's Wharf near Suffolk. That will take us all of tomorrow. We will stay the night there, and I do not think we should have trouble arranging for river transport the next day to Hampton. Today is Monday. We should be there by sometime Wednesday night, or Thursday at the latest. My crew should be arriving by the weekend. From there, depending on the weather, it will likely take us about a week to sail to Boston, same for the return trip, so we will let Charles know he should be expecting us back in about two to three weeks, or possibly a little longer if we have bad weather."

"He was worried about months," Adam said. "I reckon he'll be relieved to know it won't take as long as he was thinking."

"Time will still pass slowly for him because he is worried, but it will go by quickly for us while we are traveling. *Tan solo que Dios nos ayude con el tiempo.*" Santiago crossed himself.

"What?" Adam asked. "I understood the *Dios* part."

"Let us just pray we have good weather," his father said with a chuckle.

"By the way, I've been meaning to mention this to you,

but you know we all call him Charles Jr., right? Not Charles. Old Charles was his father."

"But Old Charles is dead now, *verdad*?" Santiago said.

Adam nodded.

"Well, he is a man. His father is dead. There is no other Charles here, so to me he is just Charles. If he likes to be called something else, he can tell me, but if he complains, I may start calling him Carlito, so *así es*." He grinned.

The barmaid returned with their drinks and food.

Adam said a quick blessing and they ate their supper. They were both so tired and hungry, they didn't take the time to casually enjoy their meal, but rather they gobbled it up as if it would be taken away from them if they didn't eat fast enough.

When they were finished, Adam had to comment. "Well, I ate it all, but I didn't like it nearly as much as Aunt Franny's food."

"I remember," Santiago said with an air of nostalgia. "She always was such a good cook."

"Still is."

"Oh, Adam, there is one thing I need to tell you," Santiago said.

"What's that?"

"Once we meet up with *La Dama* in Hampton, I will not be able to show you any special treatment just because you are my son."

"Of course not. I wouldn't expect you to."

"What you need to understand is that my crew does not know that we will be leaving right away from Hampton to sail to Boston. And they are *not* going to be pleased with that."

"Why? You can pay them for the extra time, right?"

"Yes, I can do that, at least if they stay with us for the full voyage, but they will not like the sudden change of plans, nor will they like waiting to get paid. As I explained, they are mostly new to sailing with me, and when they hear we are now going to New England, they might not trust that I will pay them as agreed upon."

"Well, just pay them all along," Adam said.

Santiago shook his head and laughed. "No, *mijo*. This is not done. A captain does not pay his crew until the voyage is done. Otherwise, what would keep them committed to finishing the trip? What if they decide they like some place halfway around the world and then they decide to stay there and not sail with you anymore? How will you get back to your home port? Most captains will keep the crew working on the ship while in port so there is no opportunity to disappear, and they will have no use for the money until they get home, anyway."

"Seems like Captain Phillips paid us something and let us go into town when we first got to Havana last year."

"That may be true," his father said. "But just think of all the trouble you got into with that." He gave Adam a sly grin. "Anyway, I suspect things may have been different, because didn't you tell me that everyone knew you wanted to look for your father there? And you do not know what your grandfather told Capt. Phillips. He might have said you should be allowed to explore there since you are his apprentice as a merchant and not necessarily a sailor's apprentice."

"Maybe so," said Adam.

"My point is that there will be no special treatment on *La Dama*, and you must avoid anything that might irritate them further. They are already going to be unhappy with the change of plans, the cold weather in the north, and then bringing Will Jr. back. I hope he will not mind sleeping in the steerage, or he is even welcome to stay in the *castillo de proa* if he is adventurous. There are only two bunks in the cabin. One is for me, of course, and the other is for Beto, the mate."

"What is *castillo de proa*?"

"I think you call it the fo'c'sle. For us it is the castle of the prow."

"I see." That amused Adam a little bit. He never thought of the forecastle as castle-like at all.

"We should probably retire early tonight. We will need to leave first thing in the morning," said Santiago.

"How about if I ask around about hiring a coach for tomorrow? Or see if anybody is heading in the same direction so we can maybe travel along?"

Santiago squinted one eye and cocked his head to the side in skepticism. "Are you sure you should be the one to do that? Remember last time you tried to hire a man to take you to parts unknown?"

Adam was annoyed that his father had said that. It already bothered him that he had made the joke about what would've happened if he hadn't left the ship in Havana, but then to make that comment. Why? Did his father wish he hadn't come looking for him when he was there? Because maybe then he wouldn't have been shot, and he wouldn't have almost died, and he wouldn't have felt like he had to come back to Beaufort.

"You know what?" Adam started to say something about it, but he decided it would probably be best if he didn't. He had a hard time envisioning how that conversation would go well, and Charles Jr. and Annabelle didn't need them to be distracted with discord right now. "I think I'll probably just go on upstairs to bed, then."

Chapter Eleven

ADAM WAS BARELY ABLE TO sleep. His mind wouldn't let him rest. He kept thinking about everything that had happened in the last few days. He had come away on what was supposed to just be a quick trip to New Bern to have some time to visit with his father, but now they had both been pulled into these circumstances with Charles Jr. and Annabelle, with no clear end in sight.

And to make matters worse, as much as he hated to admit it to himself, right now he was really thinking it might've been a bad idea convincing his father to come to Edenton.

He wished he had his journal. Sometimes writing things down helped him think through them better. As it was, he had too many thoughts jumbling around in his brain, and he couldn't think clearly.

When morning came, Adam didn't feel like he had been able to sleep for more than an hour, two at the most. This was going to be a long, *long* day.

He and his father and Charles Jr. quickly got dressed and grabbed their things, and they left the tavern. After having a breakfast of tea and oatmeal, they took off for Mr.

King's residence. Adam wished the shops were open. He really missed having his journal and when he thought about having to travel such a long distance with his father and his Spanish-speaking crew, he knew he'd need someplace to put his thoughts down. He decided to buy himself a new journal and pencil just as soon as he had an opportunity.

When they arrived at Mr. King's residence, it was around seven o'clock.

Adam sensed Charles Jr. wasn't at all comfortable with the situation. A part of him wanted to convince him to come north with him and his father, but he knew Charles Jr. would be even less comfortable with that. He'd want to be close to Annabelle to keep an eye on things—as much as possible, anyway. Also, Charles Jr.'s presence might end up being yet another thing for the crew of *La Dama* to get mad about.

They struggled to find anyone to take them to Virginia. Finally, Adam suggested they go talk to Mr. Vickers.

"Don't you reckon for the right price he'd be willing to do it?" he posited.

His father shrugged, then nodded in agreement.

It was a good idea, and Adam was at least glad to know he had found them transportation.

THE RIDE OUT OF EDENTON was largely uneventful—that is, until they came to the outskirts of Corapeake, a small village just south of the Virginia border. Evidently, it had rained the night before, because the road was a muddy mess. It was slow going there, which meant Adam had even more time to observe their surroundings. And what a murky, desolate place it was.

In spite of having visited many territories to conduct business for his grandfather's shipping company, Adam had never seen anything quite like the Dismal Swamp through which they were now traveling.

He had heard stories about it, including that wild beasts like bears, wolves, and panthers at one time or another made their homes there. He was grateful they weren't traveling in the heat of the summer, because at least that meant they wouldn't likely have to contend with the *poppa-leafs* and water moccasins, after all, there was no creature upon the earth that Adam detested more than a snake.

As gloomy as this *pocosin* was, he had heard stories that the water there—especially in nearby Lake Drummond, just across the Virginia border—was some of the purest in the world. Sailors would take barrels of the amber-colored water on sea voyages because it was said to not only resist going stagnant but to have nearly magical healing properties.

Adam and his father didn't talk much on the way to Suffolk, although Adam would have been the first to admit it wasn't for Santiago's lack of trying. His father made frequent attempts to bring up one topic or another, but Adam just didn't feel like talking. He was so tired, and he also worried about how the rest of this journey would go, especially once they met up with his father's sloop.

As they bumped along the muddy path in the carriage, Adam wondered if they would ever make it to through the miles and miles of wet, sunless, vine-choked woods. Something about traveling here reminded him the warning Dante received as he entered the gates of Hell, "Abandon all hope, ye who enter here."

He had a sinking feeling that things would only get worse the farther away from home they were.

Since he wouldn't engage in conversation, Adam realized his father was changing his tack. Instead of asking his son questions that resulted in terse answers, he began talking about his boyhood in Cuba, the games he liked to play, his first sailing trip, and the interesting people he had grown up around in Havana.

Adam's only engagement with the attempt at conversation was the occasional mumbled "Huh," or "Mmm-hmm."

No wonder my mother fancied him, Adam thought. *He loves to talk—just like she does!*

Adam willfully ignored the fact that anyone back home in Beaufort who might be asked to describe him would likely use words like "chatty," "gabby," or just plain "talkative."

The more Adam resisted conversation, the more extraordinary his father's stories became, until somewhere just a few miles south of Suffolk, as they were finally making their way into something that resembled civilization, Adam reacted to something he had just said.

"That never happened!" he told his father.

Santiago raised his eyebrows and let out a "Ha! So, you are listening!"

Adam rolled his eyes upward, then sighed. "I'm half-asleep, but yes, of course I'm listening. How could I not be listening? And I still say *that* never happened."

The *that* to which Adam was referring was an incident in a story that Santiago recounted about the time he and the crew of *La Dama* engaged in a battle and killed several men while sailing between the Philippines and Malaysia. He told how a crazed group of Iranun pirates tried to overtake his vessel. He explained how he and his crew fought bravely and how they ultimately defeated the ruffians, and sunk their vessel, sending them to the bottom of the Sulu Sea.

Adam just didn't believe it.

"Fine," said Santiago. "Ask your friend Martín next time you see him. He will tell you."

Adam wrinkled his forehead and gave his father a skeptical look. "What? What are you talking about?"

"It was the night before we found each other in Havana. I was in the ruins of el Torreón de la Chorrera with my old friend Thomas Drake and your friend Martín and some of the other men, and we were drinking whisky and talking about our most memorable times. I told about how that was the only time I had ever killed a man. But like I said, they were pirates."

"What were you doing sailing between the Philippines and Malaysia? That's on the other side of the world, for goodness' sake!"

"I have been almost anywhere you could imagine, *mijo*. When your mother and I had to part ways after the invasion at Beaufort, I was…" He rubbed his fingers in the air as if that might help him remember. "How do you say it?… Restless. I was very restless. I spent much of the time for years becoming a merchant *mundial*."

"*Mundial?*" Adam wondered aloud.

"I was a merchant of the world. How do you think it is that when you first met me at your Laney Martin's dock that I had the little things from all over the place?"

Adam thought back. He did remember that experience. He didn't know the Spanish captain of the ship that had come to Emmanuel's "second" dock at Laney Martin's estate was actually his father, and the captain didn't know that Adam was his son, but still, the meeting left an impression on him.

After Emmanuel's crew had finished helping the crew of *La Dama* unload their clandestine cargo into the cellar, Captain Velasquez invited the men to shop in the little store of exotic wares he had set up on his ship.

He had noticed Adam watching the other men browse through his wares. He asked him if he was going to buy anything and Adam responded with, "Oh, no thank you." The captain realized that the boy probably didn't have any money, so he grabbed a small cloth sack and filled it with some candies and fireworks, and then he gave it to Adam.

"*Toma esto,*" said the captain. "I think you will like these."

Adam protested at first. After all, he couldn't pay for any of that.

The captain smiled at him. "*No te preocupes. No te cobro nada.* You can have them. You worked very hard today. Everyone should go away with something."

Adam took the gift with gratitude and Captain Velasquez was unaware that one of the little items he had put in the bag ended up saving his son's life just a short time later at Richard Rasquelle's warehouse.

That one memory caused a wave of nostalgia to crash over Adam like a wave. It was as if he were seventeen again and had only recently been made an apprentice. He thought back to how he felt then. He remembered how he always wished he'd grown up with a father.

"Then you really have been all the way to China?" Adam asked.

Santiago smiled and nodded. "More than once. And

England, France, Italy, many places in Europe, the Mediterranean. So many places."

"Did you enjoy it?"

Santiago looked thoughtful before he gave a nod. "*Sí*. I did enjoy it. It gave me something to stay busy, and to keep myself from thinking too much. I tried to go to many different places because it made me spend much time learning, and I had to pay attention to where I was going, so I was not thinking all the time about leaving your mother—and you—behind."

"Why did you ever go back to Havana, then? You could have just spent your life sailing around the world."

"Yes, I could have, but I had to come back at least a couple of times each year to make sure my mother was fine." Santiago looked at Adam and raised an eyebrow. "You do not think your mother would be upset if you sailed away and never returned?"

Adam shrugged and nodded in agreement. "You're right. Had you been traveling far away shortly before we arrived in Havana last year?"

Santiago shook his head. "No, not too far. I had been to Charleston just before I arrived in Beaufort, and then I went to Philadelphia and Providence, and then Boston, to deliver some things. After all of that, I went back to Havana and decided to just rest for a while. After I left all those years ago, I would only go to Beaufort once every couple of years, and every time I went, I would always leave very sad. I would know you were there and your mother, but I could not see you or let you know I was close. Emmanuel would tell me how you were, though, so I am at least grateful for that."

"You said you went to Boston on that trip?" Adam asked.

His father nodded.

"This is your first trip back there since then, isn't it?"

He nodded again.

"But at least you have contacts there, right? That should help."

Santiago grinned. "Haha… We will see. Somehow I suspect that the people I usually do business with in Boston are moving in different circles than these people that you know."

"Catherine's family? I've never met them. Her father was a merchant, though, like Emmanuel, so I imagine you might know some of the same people."

His father shrugged. "Who knows? It is possible, I suppose."

WHEN THEY ARRIVED IN SUFFOLK, Mr. Vickers took them straight to the only place he knew in town—an inn near the Nansemond River. Part of the arrangement Adam had made with Mr. Vickers was to pay for his food and lodging in Virginia that night, and breakfast the next morning, since it would be too much for his horses to make a return trip the same day.

Their husky driver sat at the table with them to eat supper. He gobbled up everything that was set before him in a hurry and didn't say much. What little he did say came between alternating mouthfuls of bread and stew, right hand, then left, right hand again.

As soon as his belly was full, he looked at Adam and said, "Well, I reckon I need to go walk a bit." He leaned forward and added in a whisper, "Got to break wind, and I reckon I ought not do it here at the table."

Santiago just raised his eyebrows in surprise. He gave a

little nod and waved his hand forward as if to say, *Yes, by all means go.* As soon as Mr. Vickers turned and walked towards the door of the establishment, Adam couldn't help but shake his head and silently laugh.

Santiago was also a little bit amused. "That is what we would call a *sinvergüenza,*" he said to Adam.

"What does that mean?"

"He has no shame!"

Father and son shared a laugh. Then Santiago said, "You make sure you always use good manners."

Adam nodded. "I do try to, though I reckon I might slip a little bit from time to time."

Santiago shook his head. "No, do not say you try to have good manners. You *must* have good manners. People will judge you for that, and they will laugh at your expense if you do not. For instance, if you eat so fast with strangers, as this man did, or if you talk about such things as breaking wind, it reflects poorly on you, but it also reflects poorly on your family, who raised you."

At this point, Adam was ready to change the subject, but apparently his father was not.

"Listen, son, I have not been able to oversee your upbringing. I do not know exactly how your mother raised you in that tavern, or what habits you may be learning from the men back at the shipping company, but I will tell you now, you should always be mindful of your *reputación.* Otherwise, you might be the one they call *sinvergüenza.*"

What in the world? Adam thought. *How did we end up on this?* Adam hoped his father wasn't about to start trying to pack nearly twenty years of father-son instruction into just a few short days.

Just then his father changed the subject, as if he were reading Adam's mind.

"You said you have never been to Hampton Roads, *verdad?*"

Adam shook his head. "No, never had cause to go there. Most of my traveling has just been up to New Bern or Bath, except for that trip to Havana."

"Do you enjoy sailing?"

Adam shrugged. "I like it just fine, but I don't know that I'd want to be at sea as much as someone like you, or Emmanuel's usual crew."

"Is that so?" asked Santiago. "I thought you might enjoy the adventure, seeing new places."

"I do. I do enjoy that," said Adam. He chuckled. "But to be honest, I'm not that fond of sharing such close quarters with a bunch of stinking men for weeks on end. Maybe it's because I was raised by a woman and I didn't grow up with brothers."

"Well, as his apprentice, what is your grandfather preparing you to do at Rogers's Shipping Company?"

"He's had me learning a little bit of everything. When I first started working there, I was trained by Boaz on the essential skills of coopering. I'm not expected to become a master cooper, but he wanted me familiar enough with the trade so that I can help when needed. The next year, of course, was when he sent me to Havana. Since I returned from that trip, he's had me doing everything, from helping manage the books, to conducting business with customers, to taking inventory, and so forth."

Santiago leaned back in his chair before asking, "Has he ever mentioned making you captain of the *Gypsy?*"

Adam shook his head. "No, of course we don't need a new captain. Carl Phillips is a good, reliable captain, and when he's no longer able to captain the *Gypsy*, I reckon his little brother, Charlie, will do it."

"Would you like to learn how to captain a ship?"

"Eh..." Adam tipped his head to the side. "I know it would be a good skill to have, but I really can't see when I'd need to use it."

"There is good money to be made when you are able to captain your own ship, make your own business arrangements, sail for yourself, not for a merchant *patrón*, although I do not doubt that Emmanuel would be a fair man to work for."

"I would hope so," said Adam with a half grin. "Knowing what I know now, I would hope his concern for me would go beyond my apprenticeship bond."

"I am not asking you these things to just make conversation, *mijo*. I want you to know that if you ever want to learn to captain your own ship, I can teach you on *La Dama*. She will be yours one day, you know?"

"Hmm..." Adam looked pensive. "I remember what your will said when I was in Havana. But do you really think your ship will last longer than you?"

Santiago chuckled. "I hope I live a very long time, but the day will come when I will be too old to sail her, even if that is not for many years. I am not quite an old man yet, after all."

"You're not even yet forty years old!" said Adam.

"Yes, I know this, but *sin embargo* I will not be able to sail always. When the time comes that I am too old, if you do not wish to sail *La Dama*, then I should make other arrangements to allow her to continue in this business. She is made of the best cedar, like your grandfather's ship. Both *La Dama* and the *Gypsy* should last a very long time—many, many more years than the oak-built ships."

"To be honest," said Adam, "I'd be happy to finish my apprenticeship, secure a regular position with Emmanuel at the shipping company, and then get married and raise a family."

"Those are noble goals," said Santiago. "You would do well to achieve those things, and of course you will, but if you ever change your mind about learning how to command a ship, I will be glad to train you."

"I'll remember that," said Adam.

THE NEXT MORNING, ADAM AND his father again had breakfast with Mr. Vickers before seeing him off on his way back to Edenton. The father-and-son pair wouldn't have to be in a particular hurry. They could get to Hampton anytime before tomorrow and still have plenty of time to meet up with La Dama.

Once they left the inn, they went right down to the wharf to find out how they would travel to Hampton. They found a periauger that reserved seats for passengers. They made arrangements with the master. The boat would be leaving in about an hour, so they had a few minutes if they needed any last-minute items before the daylong sail.

Adam told his father he wanted to see if he could find a shop that sold writing supplies. Meanwhile, Santiago said he would try to find a place where he might be able to buy some foul-weather gear—at least some extra wool socks and oiled canvas coats.

"That's a good idea," said Adam. When he and his father had first left Beaufort for New Bern, they didn't anticipate being gone more than a couple of days, so they hadn't brought more than a single change of clothes with them. They certainly wouldn't have anticipated the colder temperatures they would be facing farther north.

Adam went to the general store, which was just a few steps away from the wharf. He knew they should have blank books and pencils. He chose a small book with a leather cover that he could tie with a cord to keep closed. It was almost identical to the one he had back in his room at the shipping company, only this one would fit in his coat pocket.

He got back to the dock before his father did. A couple of other men were apparently also waiting for the trip upriver. The master of the periauger started down the dock towards them, and Adam got nervous about whether his father would make it back in time. He was nowhere to be seen. Fortunately, just before it was time to go, Santiago came running towards the dock carrying a big wrapped bundle.

"Were you able to find the things?" Adam asked.

Santiago nodded. "Two coats, four pairs of *calcetines de lana*, and two shirts. They are not the best I have seen, and they cost a fortune, but they will be better than having nothing."

"They had *two* tarred canvas coats on hand for you to buy?"

"One of these was a model the tailor kept on hand in the store—I think it is his own coat—and the other he had recently made for another man. I tell you, that man will not be happy when he comes to get his coat and the tailor tells him he has to make another one."

Adam's eyes were big and he shook his head. "No, I don't reckon he will. You paid right much for these, then."

Santiago nodded. His expression made it evident that the transaction was a costly one.

Adam assumed that second item his father had mentioned, *cal-say-teen* whatevers, were socks, because that was the only thing his father had planned to buy other than the coats. He asked, though, just to be sure.

"Yes," Santiago said. "*Calcetines* are socks. You will be speaking *español* before this whole journey is over, I think."

"Maybe so." Adam chuckled.

Soon he and his father, along with the master and two boys not much younger than Adam, whom Adam assumed were the man's sons and crew, and the other two passengers were on board the long open boat, with two large barrels fastened with straps, making their way up the Nansemond River. The trip to Hampton would take the whole day. It was already going to be an uncomfortable voyage with the brisk and windy weather, but when a misty rain started about an hour upriver, things turned miserable. It would have been even worse if they didn't have with them their new foul-weather coats.

"I don't care how much they were," said Adam. "These coats were worth whatever you paid for them! And it's not even that cold here!"

Santiago nodded in agreement. The other two passengers didn't have the same kinds of coats, but they didn't seem bothered by it. They were content to sit with something that looked like a large piece of sailcloth pulled over their heads.

"You know, I will have to spend much more money when we get to Hampton," Santiago said loudly over the wind and rain. "I am thinking about it, and my crew is unlikely to have enough of the very-cold-weather coats for being on deck."

"They won't?" Adam shouted in response.

Santiago shook his head. "No. Like I said, this new crew is mostly accustomed to the warm weather in the Caribe."

After they had battled periods of torrential rain, followed by brief reprieves, they reached the mouth of the Nansemond. Adam was relieved that it appeared they had put the storms completely behind them. As they made their approach to enter Hampton Roads—a large natural harbor where the Nansemond, the James, and the Elizabeth Rivers come together—they began to see ships of all shapes and size coming and going in every direction. To Adam, it was an impressive sight.

Once they finally docked at Hampton, it was almost ten o'clock.

THEY WERE HAPPY THE MASTER of the periauger was able to direct them to a tavern that would still let rooms to guests even at that late hour. After they checked in, they were able to enjoy a meal from the kitchen before retiring to their shared room. They both slept hard that night, as it was the first decent opportunity either of them had gotten to do that since they left Beaufort.

The next day was Thursday, and *La Dama* might arrive as soon as Friday or Saturday. Santiago and Adam stopped by the warehouse for the merchant where *La Dama* would be making its delivery and let him know they were in town and where they could be found when the ship arrived.

The two were fortunately able to find enough decent cold-weather clothing, including thick woolens, canvas coats, and wool thrum caps, for the new men of the crew, as well as some new items for the longtime members, just to acknowledge their seniority. Santiago said he was trying to think ahead and avoid as many *broncas*, which Adam understood to mean "fights" or "problems," as possible.

It seemed like everything was falling right into place when Santiago and Adam went by the warehouse where *La Dama* was expected to arrive anyday and found she was already there and the crew was in the process of moving the cargo to the dock.

When Filiberto caught sight of his *capitán*, he strode purposefully over to speak to him. Santiago proceeded to present Adam to the ship's mate in Spanish, and then he explained to Adam who Filiberto was and that he had been sailing with him for many years. He then said a few more things to Filiberto in Spanish and excused him to oversee the crew.

Once he was out of earshot, Santiago explained to Adam that his nickname was "Beto" and that he took his job very seriously. *Very* seriously. In other words, of everyone on the crew, Beto was not someone he wanted to joke around with.

"But," Santiago explained, "I would trust him with my life. And he knows what honor means." He also told Adam about how Beto used to be second mate, and his first mate was Alonso Cordova, nicknamed Poncho, which was a name that would be familiar to Adam from his trip to Cuba. Sadly, Poncho was now deceased.

"Who is the second mate now?" Adam asked.

"Ah, that would be Beto's brother, Miguel. He is also a good man. I have known both of them almost my whole life."

"Well, at least you have two men you can trust in those roles," said Adam.

"That is true. And Poncho's son is sailing with us now. He is one of the new members. He joined *La Dama* when he learned that I was coming to Carolina. He wanted to escape from his mother, *la borrachita*, and her new husband, *el bruto*. He is a couple of years older than you, I think."

"I can figure out what *bruto* means, but what about *borrachita*?"

"She likes to drink," Santiago said. "It is a very sad thing."

"Oh... I see. Well, does he speak any English?" Adam asked.

Santiago shook his head. "I do not know, but since you will be sailing together, maybe you can teach each other your own native languages."

"We can surely try," said Adam. He made an effort to remember the names he had learned so far. "Alright, there's you, the captain, Beto, the first mate, Tony, the cook, and what did you say Poncho's son's name is?"

"His name is Francisco, but we call him Paco."

"Paco? How do you get Paco from Francisco?"

Santiago chuckled and then shrugged. "I do not know, but that is what we say. That is a short name for Francisco."

"Haha, if you say so," said Adam. "Who is the bosun?"

"We call that our *contramaestre*. He is one of our new men, Ernesto," Santiago said. "We are lucky to have him. He is very knowledgeable. He has been serving as *contramaestre* on different ships around the Spanish West Indies for many years, and in fact he helped me recruit the rest of the deck-hands for the new crew of *La Dama*."

Just a few hours later, Santiago and Adam had retrieved the few things they had left at the tavern and boarded the vessel. There was one member of the crew who was able to speak limited conversational English, and that was the sloop's cook, Antonio, or, as everyone called him, Tony. He had also been with the crew for years.

Santiago instructed Tony to accompany Adam and Ernesto, the boatswain, around the vessel so Ernesto could instruct Adam on all of his tasks for being part of the crew, and Tony could translate. They also had to show him which bunk he'd be able to use in the forecastle, along with letting him know his schedule and the watch rotation.

This was going to be interesting. Adam was already intimidated by the fact that the whole crew would be operating in Spanish, but it was also evident that his father ran a much tighter ship than Captain Phillips did on the *Gypsy*.

Chapter Twelve

A DAM'S FIRST MORNING AT SEA on *La Dama* began
with the boatswain's wake-up call. It took him a few
seconds after he opened his eyes for it to dawn on him
where he was. The other deckhands—at least the ones who
weren't just finishing their watch—were tumbling out of
their bunks and shuffling about hurriedly to get ready to
report on deck to begin a new workday.

Tony explained to him in his choppy English that he
should hurry up and eat, because he'd need to be up top and
helping to scrub the decks in short order.

This was very different from the *Gypsy*, Adam thought,
but not necessarily in a bad way. The crew of the *Gypsy* acted
more like one big family, while this crew was very structured
and disciplined. And Adam was beginning to understand
exactly what his father meant about not showing him any
special treatment.

Over the course of the week it took them to sail to Boston,
Adam got to know the personalities of each of the crew members, even if he wasn't really able to communicate with them
effectively. Fortunately, shipboard tasks were universal, so he

caught on quickly to the Spanish terms for things he already knew how to do.

He had definitely formed his opinions about the men whom he was sailing with. The first and second mates, even though they were brothers, were as different as night and day. Beto, the first mate, was every bit as serious as Adam's father had said he was, but his brother, Miguel, on the other hand, was a joker. His more laid-back form of leadership on this otherwise rigidly run ship was something Adam appreciated.

On the other hand, there were a couple of deckhands with whom he occasionally had to work—Ignacio, whom everyone called Nacho, and Joaquín—who he always felt were talking about him behind his back. They'd say things to each other, then occasionally make movements with their hands, then sometimes sneak glances at him and laugh as though they'd just told a joke at his expense. If Miguel was leading the crew on their watch, he'd always say something to them about it, which Adam appreciated, even though he didn't understand any of it.

Adam much preferred working alongside Paco, the son of the late Alfonso Cordova, and Rafael, better known as Rafa, who was not only a deckhand but also the ship's carpenter.

They were fortunate from the time they had left Hampton to have the winds and currents working in their favor, even if the weather was increasingly cold—that is, until they rounded Nantucket. It was then that they began to go through several bands of rain, until finally, as they sailed past Provincetown, they were pounded by a steady downpour that lasted all the way to Boston. Adam did have experience sailing through strong storms thanks to the hurricane through which they sailed on his voyage to Havana. The difference this time was that the weather was biting cold, and that, coupled with rain, made for miserable conditions that called for all hands on deck.

Adam sincerely hoped by the time they found Will and were on their way back to North Carolina these storms would have passed.

Chapter Thirteen

As they came into the harbor at Boston, Adam was impressed to see the wide variety of ships. Hampton had been quite a sight, but this was different. Something about the scene reminded him of Havana, though he couldn't put his finger on what it was.

Seeing so many vessels of every shape and size, coupled with the backdrop of a bustling city, was something to which he wasn't very accustomed.

They sailed just north of what was called the Long Wharf and then docked at one of the smaller wharfs halfway between that one and another one, called Hancock's. There was a large warehouse just up from the dock, but they wouldn't be unloading cargo there. Instead, Santiago explained to Adam that the building belonged to an old friend, who might be able to help them find the home where the Martins would be staying.

Santiago gave his crew instructions, and then he spoke to the boatswain and pointed at some of the lines, which had been badly chafed during the storm. Adam didn't understand exactly what he said, but he could tell his father was talking to Ernesto about fixing them.

Santiago then pointed to Adam and gruffly motioned for him to follow him, which he did.

"Do the crew understand why I'm leaving the ship with you here?" Adam asked.

"Beto knows. It is up to him to inform others as needed. This is the place that I told you about." Santiago pointed to the building they were approaching. "I have done business here many times."

They hurriedly walked up the dock to a warehouse, which looked like it hadn't been used in some time. It was a strange thing to see. As busy as the harbor was, it didn't seem likely that there would be any vacancies on the waterfront. One would think any available warehouse would be occupied with productive work of loading and unloading shipments.

Santiago looked confused as they ran to what was the main door of the warehouse and tried to enter. The door was locked. He knocked, but there was no answer. It wasn't surprising, since the building looked abandoned.

"Oy!" yelled a tall, lanky man of about thirty or so from a building across the street. "Wot you need, mate? Can I 'elp ya wif somefin?"

Adam and his father crossed the street to speak to him. As they got to the building, the man motioned for them to come in out of the rain, so they did. His clothes looked work-worn and his hair was a limp, greasy mess. Adam didn't see a sign for what business was at that building, but he had to wonder after seeing this fellow. What kind of place would it be for him to look so ragged?

"I am looking for Mr. Letchworth," said Santiago. He

grabbed the collar of his coat and gave it a good shake to knock some of the rain off. "Do you know him?"

The man nodded. "I did, God rest 'is soul, but 'e died 'bout a monf ago and 'is 'eirs is quibblin 'bout wot to do wif 'is place so ve administratah of ve estate shuh' it all down till vey can get it all sor'ed."

Adam and his father exchanged a concerned look, and then Santiago took a deep breath and sighed before asking the man, "What of Mr. Conley?"

"'Oo?" the man asked.

"Mr. Conley was Mr. Letchworth's assistant. You must know who he is." Santiago raised his hand to just below his own height and said, "He was about this tall, with bright-red hair and a big round belly and very thin legs like two sticks. You would know him if you saw him."

The man shook his head. "Ah, prob'ly nevah did, ven. Nevah saw anybo'y like vat. Ven again, I ain't been 'ere much longah van a year or two, so might be 'e wuz gone 'fore I came."

"I see." Santiago looked like he was thinking for a moment, then stamped in frustration and motioned to Adam to follow him. "Thank you for your help," he said as they were walking away. He turned to his son. "I know another place we can get help."

They crossed the street, and Adam noticed a sign said they were on Fish Street. They continued south along the waterfront, and when they were well out of the man's earshot, his father said, "He is *un criado ligado por contrato*. He cannot help us."

"What?" Adam asked.

"He is a servant who is bound to service, like a contract."

"An indentured servant?"

"*Sí*. You could not tell he is from London?"

"Sure," said Adam, "but so are a lot of people. That doesn't mean he's—"

"He looks *terrible*, and when we were crossing over to the building, I noticed there was a rich man looking out the upstairs window of that building at us—probably his master—and he looked *impatiente*."

"Why would it have to be his master? Might've just been his boss," said Adam.

They were walking as quickly as possible because of the rain.

"No, *lo dudo*," said Santiago. "The man obviously has no money, and he certainly did not grow up here, so how do you think he came to Boston?"

Adam shrugged. "Maybe he came on one of those ships in the harbor. Men do that all the time, don't they?"

"He came on one of those ships, but on that other man's purse," said Santiago. "Now he will work for him until his *contrato* is complete."

It was an interesting theory, thought Adam, and definitely a possibility, but it annoyed him that his father not only assumed that the man was an indentured servant, but also that his father thought he was too blind to see that it was the case. Also, he thought it was shortsighted of his father to assume the man could offer them no help, given the circumstances. After all, he might've known the Wells family.

Santiago said they should turn once they came to the next street. They did, and within a block they reached a two-story tavern with a sign that reminded Adam of the Topsail, as both designs suggested their typical patrons were sailors and fishermen—only the Topsail Tavern featured a single-masted sloop, while this one featured a full-rigged ship.

They entered a familiar setting. It seemed—to Adam at least—that taverns for seafaring types must be nearly all the same. Maybe different architecture and different accents, but the clientele, with their tanned, stubbly faces that looked like old leather, and the loud chatter felt like home to him. The air smelled of tobacco and rum, and the heavy aroma of yeasty bread hung thick in the air along with the lingering scent of salt water that had been sun-baked into the men's clothing and hair.

A man busily pouring drinks called out to them from behind the bar, "Sit wherever you can find a seat. Be right with you."

Adam and his father found a table very near the door. It wasn't a particularly cozy spot, as the opening and closing of the door made for a terrible draft. It was a good thing they'd kept their coats on rather than leaving them on the wall hooks at the entrance.

"I reckon they're shorthanded," Adam remarked. He knew that was generally the case if Valentine was serving tables at the Topsail Tavern.

"Maybe he is just too cheap to hire servers," Santiago joked.

"You've come to this place many times before?" asked Adam.

"Yes, but it has been a few years. Seems different now. I do not recognize that man at the bar."

"Maybe they have new owners."

"Perhaps," said Santiago.

Just then, the fat-bellied man came over towards them.

He was wiping his hands on a bar mop, and then he flipped it up on his shoulder.

"How can I help you gentlemen today?" said the man

"You take care of this whole place by yourself?" Santiago said.

"We usually have more staff in here, but with the meeting happening in the upstairs room, they're all tending to that crowd."

"A meeting?" Santiago wondered aloud.

"About the damned taxes," said the barkeep. "They're always about the damned taxes."

Adam nodded knowingly.

Santiago didn't react one way or another. Instead, he said, "Do you have Madeira?"

The barkeep nodded.

"I will have that, and also whatever you recommend from your kitchen."

"How about some clam chowder and bread? I'm afraid the offerings are limited with the crowd upstairs."

Santiago nodded. "That will be fine."

"I'll have cider," said Adam. "And the chowder is fine for me too."

The barkeep gave him a nod, then left the table to go tend to their order.

"You going to ask the man if any of the people you know still work here?"

"I will, but when we pay our bill."

"And if none of those people are still here?"

Santiago furrowed his brow. "You know the name of this family, yes?"

Adam nodded. "Well, I know that Catherine was a Wells

before she married Will. And I know that her father was a big, successful merchant."

"I never knew any merchant with the name of Wells," said Santiago. "But then again, I will only know the people I have dealt with in the past, and then anyone they introduce me to—*contrabandistas todos*."

"*Contrabandistas*? Smugglers?"

Santiago grinned and gave a mischievous nod while patting the air with his hands as if to say, *Shh*.

Adam rolled his eyes and gave a little grin. "Well, you never know. Mr. Wells may do his part to fight taxes. We'll have to ask him when we see him."

"Oh sure," said Santiago with a cocked eyebrow and a laugh.

After they ate their meal and had their drinks, they went up to the bar, and Santiago paid the barkeep.

"Sir, before we leave, I wanted to ask you: Does Mr. Carney still own this place?"

The barkeep shook his head. "No. In fact, the place has had a new owner for about a year now."

"I see," said Santiago. "Perhaps you can help us. I was wondering if you might know where we can find some friends. They are in town visiting an old Boston family, but we do not know where they live."

"An old Boston family? Who are they?" He proceeded to take down mugs from a shelf and fix drinks for some recently arrived patrons.

"We're looking for the Wells family. Mr. Wells is a shipping merchant. His daughter Catherine and son-in-law, Will Martin, are friends of ours from North Carolina, and we need to find them here in town."

"Wells, huh?" The man behind the bar held up a finger for them to wait a moment while he delivered the drinks to a nearby table. He returned behind the bar and said, "You know, I can't remember anybody by the name of Wells. Then again, I might not have met him. Depends on the kind of fellow this Mr. Wells is." He waved his hands in the air. "Would he come to a place like this? Because I've always worked in taverns like this one."

Adam was amused at the man's comment, since it was basically the same kind of thing his father had said. It made him wonder what kind of man Mr. Wells might be.

"We don't know," said Adam. "We've never met him. But I get the sense he's well-off—very successful."

"Then it ain't likely he'd be hanging around here, is it? Unless he's a kindler."

"A kindler?" Santiago said.

The barkeep stuck his thumb upwards. "I mean like those fellows upstairs."

"Ah, I see."

"Do you know anyone who might know who he is? Maybe someone who knows the merchants around here."

"You mean other than the obvious?"

Adam and Santiago knew who he was talking about. A natural choice would be to ask one of His Majesty's revenue collectors, but the last thing they wanted to do was go hunting for a tax man, especially with Santiago's obvious Spanish provenance.

"Yes, can you think of anyone?" Santiago asked.

"There's a young fellow sitting over there at that table." The man pointed towards a boy of about fourteen or so sitting at a small table right next to the stairs that led to the second floor. "Go ask him. I bet if anybody knows, he will."

Santiago wrinkled his brow. "You mean that child?"

"I'd ask him if it were me. He's an apprentice to one of those men upstairs. He'll know about men involved in shipping around here."

Adam didn't doubt for one minute what the barkeep had suggested. He knew that if that boy was involved in that business as an apprentice, there was every likelihood he'd know about most local merchants, even if only by name, regardless of his age.

Santiago was skeptical. He apparently didn't want to be made a fool of, so he said to Adam, "You go over there and see if you can find anything out from the boy. You are not much older than him. I will wait for you outside."

Adam nodded. He was happy to see what he could find out from the boy, and yet aggravated that his father apparently thought it beneath him to try to get useful information from someone so young.

He went over to the boy's table and motioned to the chair. "Hello there. My name's Adam Fletcher." He reached out to greet the boy.

The young man shook his hand. "I'm Tom Elder."

"Nice to make your acquaintance, Tom Elder."

"Likewise."

"Mind if I sit down?"

"Be my guest," the boy said.

Adam sat down. "That fellow over there said you're the man I'll want to talk to if I need to find out about a local merchant."

The boy looked pleased that he'd been recommended.

"Who'd that be? I know every merchant—on this end of town, at least."

"Do you know a man called Mr. Wells?"

The young man scrunched up his face. "Mr. Wells? Hmm…" He looked pensive. "Name's familiar… Hang on. Yes, I know who Mr. Wells is. Well, more accurately, I *knew* Mr. Wells. He's been dead more than a year now, I reckon."

"More than a year? Just curious, but how long have you been a merchant's apprentice?"

Tom cocked his head to the side and gave a grin. "Been around the trade my whole life. My father was a merchant, but he died when I was not quite five. I've been apprenticed to Mr. Lewis since I was eleven. I'm nearly fifteen now, so about four years as an apprentice."

"If Mr. Wells is deceased, do you happen to know where we might find his warehouse? Are they still in business?"

Tom nodded. "The building is still there, yeah, but another man runs his business at the place. Not sure what it is, though."

"How do I get there?"

Tom gave him directions that sounded very much like they would take him back in the direction of where they'd come when they first arrived in town by the docks. He thanked the boy and gave him a coin, then wished him well.

"Thank you, sir. And if you need anything else while you're in town, know that you can find me here nearly every day around this time, unless Mr. Lewis sends me on an errand."

Adam tipped his hat to the boy and bade him farewell.

WHEN THEY STEPPED OUTSIDE THE tavern, Adam and his father were both relieved there was a break in the rain.

His father asked him, "Were you able to find out anything useful?"

Adam grinned and nodded. "Yes, sir. I know right where we need to go. Follow me."

"Fine then," Santiago said with a half smile. "Lead the way."

As they started walking back in the direction from which they had come, Santiago asked, "Where exactly are we going?"

Adam chuckled. "Remember that Londoner? Well, we're going right down there. I think it might even be that exact building."

Santiago rolled his eyes. "You must be joking."

"I'm not." Adam laughed.

The cold air coming from the north cut against their faces. The men walked with their heads down, and their pace was quick. The sooner they could get to their destination, the better.

Within a short time, they were approaching the very street corner where Santiago and Adam had met the man that first spoke to them.

"It looks like they might have already gone for the day," Santiago observed.

"Ah, maybe someone will be there," Adam said.

He ran up to the front door and knocked. Santiago stood several feet back.

Soon the same man who'd spoken to them earlier came to the door.

"Ah, 'tis you again, mate. Din't expect you back 'ere so soon."

"Turns out this is right where we needed to be," Adam remarked. "We should've asked you if you knew Mr. Wells. We understand this used to be the offices for his shipping company before he died."

The man nodded. "Indeed it was, sir. May 'e rest in peace. Now me mastah, Mr. Folger, is runnin it. Doin' a fine job, too, 'e is. 'E's a good man."

"That's great to hear. Well, I was hoping you might be able to tell us where we can find the Wells home. Specifically, we're looking for the daughter and son-in-law of Mr. Wells. They are friends of ours from North Carolina and we've come to bring them news."

"News? Must be real impor'ant if you come all this way."

Adam nodded. "It is. Very important. Do you know where we might find that family?"

The man shook his head. "Wish I could 'elp ya, but I'm afraid you'll have ta wait and ask me master. 'E's gone for tha day on family business. 'E'll be 'ere bright an' early tomorrow."

"I see," said Adam. "We'll just come back, then. Mr. Folger, you said?"

"Vat's right," said the man.

"What's your name, by the way?" Adam asked. "I'm Adam Fletcher." He reached out to shake hands with the man.

"Toby. Toby Stocks."

"Nice to meet you, Toby. We'll see you in the morning, I reckon."

"Farewell," said Toby.

Adam waved goodbye, and then he went back over to speak to his father. "The Londoner's name is Toby. He knew who Mr. Wells was, but he doesn't know where he lives. He said his master, Mr. Folger, could help us, but he won't be back until the morning. I think we might as well just rest tonight and find out what we can tomorrow."

"I really do not think it is wise for us to lose much time," said Santiago.

"How much time will we lose? We can spend the next several hours searching and not have any luck finding them, but even if we do, it's unlikely Will is going to want to pack up his things and leave tonight."

"This is true," said Santiago. "You should probably just go back to *La Dama* and get some rest. We can find them first thing tomorrow. In fact, in the morning you go back to this shipping company and find out where we can find the Martins. I think I might ask around and see if anyone has anything we can take back to Carolina for a fair price. We can make a little bit of money while we are here."

Adam hadn't really had his mind on money, but it wouldn't be a bad thing if his father was able to round up some business while he was tracking down Will and family in Boston. After all, it would help offset the unexpected expenses of the trip.

The men went back to the ship, where the aroma coming up from the chimney out of the forecastle told them that Tony had already cooked supper. One thing Adam decided for sure on this voyage was that Tony's cooking ability, especially given the very limited resources he had on board, was remarkable. He was able to actually make decent-tasting food with otherwise-unappealing ingredients, a pot, and a pan.

After the crew had eaten, the second mate, Miguel, told Adam he was free to retire to his berth for the night. The crew was ordinarily used to operating with one less man, anyway, and those who would be working would just be helping the boatswain repair the lines and the sails.

Another thing about which Adam was grateful on this trip was that he had an actual bunk to sleep in, complete with a little curtain he could pull to for privacy. On the *Gypsy*, he'd only ever had a hammock.

By the warm, muted glow of his lantern, which he was able to afix to a small shelf with a peg, he began writing in his journal. He made notes about meeting the young apprentice, Tom Elder, and also the Londoner, Toby Charles. He also recorded the meal he'd eaten at the tavern and the rotund barkeep who'd served them while a meeting happened upstairs.

He wished this little book was as large as the journal he kept in his drawer back home, as he wanted to sketch some things, including a couple of the men he'd met that day, as well as that tavern. He decided he'd just do the best he could. He didn't want to forget the faces of the men who'd helped him. He also decided to make a map, tiny though it was, of the streets on which he'd traveled so far in Boston. Tomorrow, after finding out where Catherine's family lived and visiting them, he'd want to add that to the map as well.

He also made note of the overall tidiness of the ship and the orderly way in which it was run, but he was amused that in spite of everything always being otherwise shipshape, there had been a few occasions where the ship's carpenter, Rafa, had tools go missing, and other occasions where he'd find things out of place. He mused on paper that perhaps with the crew otherwise running like a well-oiled machine, something was bound to slip—in this case, the ability to keep track of necessary tools.

Finally, as he thought about the largely rootless crew, all

in search of adventure, he jotted down something he remembered from *Poor Richard's Almanack*:

I never saw an oft-transplanted tree,

Nor yet an oft-removed family,

That throve so well as those that settled be.

Chapter Fourteen

WHEN MORNING CAME, ADAM COULD hear rain pounding on the deck above his head. He dreaded having to go out again in that foul weather, but he was eagerly anticipating seeing Laney Martin again, maybe within hours.

He climbed down out of his berth and forced himself to get ready, which mostly involved changing shirts, putting on his boots and waistcoat, and running a comb through his unruly, wavy, dark hair. He pulled it back and tied it with a leather cord, then stroked his cheeks between his thumb and fingers. *I wish I had my razor*, he thought. Sadly, it was another item he'd left home without, and he hadn't felt it necessary to buy one on his travels. It occurred to him he could borrow his father's, but when he came up on deck, he found that his father had already left to tend to some business. So much for borrowing that razor.

He decided he ought not waste time and instead head right over to the Folger building so he could talk to Toby or Mr. Folger. He wondered how Charles Jr. and Annabelle were faring, then felt guilty that the first thing he'd thought about when it came to finding the Martins was that he would be seeing Laney. Meanwhile, Charles Jr. and Annabelle were still apart and probably going through hell. They had to be anxious for them to get back to Edenton with Will Martin.

Adam had only made it about twenty yards up the dock towards the street when he pulled his coat more tightly around him to fight off the wind and the rain. *I hate this weather*, he thought. It was only late October. He didn't even want to think about how cold it must get by January or February. He knew it had to be at least twenty degrees colder than it was back home—or maybe it was just the seemingly endless wind and rain that made it feel that way. *No wonder Catherine was happy to move down south!*

When he arrived at the Folger building, he at first wondered if he should knock, but it seemed like the kind of place where you let yourself in. No matter. He was eager to get out of the rain. The door was open, but he didn't see anyone in the room where he first entered. Considering it was a shipping company, Adam was surprised that there were no cargo doors—at least not that he was able to see from the front and side of the building. In fact, it looked as though there had once been cargo doors but they had been bricked over. What kind of merchants weren't going to have an easy way to bring cargo in and out? And why on earth would they brick over perfectly good doors? Rogers's Shipping Company had enormous bay doors on both the side facing Taylor Creek and the side facing the street.

There were two doors leading to other parts of the building from this room. One was directly to his left by the main entrance, while the other was on the wall directly in front of the entrance. Adam tried opening each of them, wondering if he'd find Toby or anyone else inside, but both were locked.

"Hellooo!" he called out. "It's Adam Fletcher. I've come to talk to Mr. Folger." He waited a moment or two before calling out again, this time to the Londoner. "Toby, are you here?"

He heard footsteps that sounded like they were on a flight stairs, though he couldn't make out if they were coming up or down. Then he heard the clicking of the lock in the door directly to the left of where he stood, and finally it was opened. A well-dressed, stern-looking man came through the door, closed it behind him, then locked it.

Adam wasn't sure, but he thought it was probably the man his father had seen in the upstairs window the day before—Toby's master.

"I'm Jonathan Folger. How can I help you, sir?" the man asked.

He sounded much nicer than he looked. Adam was relieved to realize he was just one of those fellows with a serious-looking face.

"Good day to you, sir." Adam reached out his hand and introduced himself before he explained, "I was talking to the man that works for you yesterday, Toby, and he said you might be able to help me find the family of the man who used to own this place, Mr. Wells."

Mr. Folger clapped his hands in surprise and said, "My goodness, are you a friend of the Wells family? I thought so highly of the gentleman, God bless his soul."

"Actually, sir," Adam explained, "I've never met anyone from the Wells family except for the daughter, Catherine. She's married to a very good friend of mine, William Martin,

Esquire, from New Bern, North Carolina. I've actually come to Boston to fetch him to tend to some business back home. That is why it's imperative that I find him today if at all possible."

Mr. Folger's countenance changed. He looked concerned having apparently detected the urgency in Adam's voice. "Oh I see. I'm happy to give you directions to the family's home, although they're no longer at the Wells place. The missus has remarried, to a Scotsman named Wallace. Good man. She did well. In any case, his place is just a little over a mile from here, in Beacon Hill, but I'd say it'd be best for you to hire a coach, especially in this torrent."

"Oh, that will be just fine, sir," said Adam. He took his journal and his pencil out of his pocket and asked for directions.

Mr. Folger wrote down the names of the nearest cross streets, then wrote the words "Large brick house. *Very* large."

"Thank you, sir. I guess I'll go try to find a coach for hire, then."

Mr. Folger raised up his index finger. "Ah, I can help with that." He motioned for Adam to follow him. He proceeded to unlock the *other* door. The one that had been directly opposite the entrance when Adam first entered the building. Adam followed him into a giant room that he imagined was once the main area for storing cargo, but now it was filled with some very large tables and sundry devices and equipment that Adam couldn't even begin to identify. They arrived at another door on the opposite side of the great space.

While Mr. Folger shuffled through a large key ring to find the key to the door, Adam's curiosity got the better of him. "Are you a merchant, sir?"

Mr. Folger tipped his head from side to side before answering, "A little bit I am, yes. Well, not exactly, really. I do have a cousin who's a merchant. I dabble in different sorts of things."

"I was wondering, because I know Mr. Wells was a very successful merchant, but when I saw the outside of your building, I noticed the spaces where bay doors would likely be had been bricked over."

"Aha! Here it is." He'd found the key he was looking for and he attempted to open the lock on the door, though he seemed to be struggling with it. "Yes, well, the thing about bay doors is they do tend to let in so much of the weather, but I very much prefer to keep it outside, where it belongs, unless it's being helpful, of course."

Finally, Adam heard the click of the lock. He was really intrigued now. What on earth was this man's profession?

"I do buy things and sell things, so in that sense, yes, I suppose I am a merchant of sorts," said Mr. Folger. "But first and foremost I'm a scientist."

Adam was surprised at that. "A scientist? Really? I've never met a scientist before."

"Well, now you have." Mr. Folger made a funny face that Adam was able to detect as a smile, strange though it was. "I like solving problems. I'm interested in different means of powering things, electricity, steam... My goodness! I've been reading about some very exciting developments of engines that run on steam. Can you imagine?"

"That sounds remarkable," said Adam. "You're an inventor, then?"

"Not just yet, though I have another cousin in

Philadelphia who's made some clever discoveries. Perhaps it runs in the family. We'll just have to wait and see."

"Well, I think if you have a great passion for science, you will eventually find success. I wonder what sort of things you'll invent."

"Lord willing, something to do with new sources of power, but first I must understand the science behind new discoveries as they are made. No need to reinvent the wheel, don't you agree?"

"Oh indeed," said Adam with a nod.

Mr. Folger opened the door that he had just unlocked and pointed across an alleyway. "See there? I've just invented a way for you to hire a coach without walking far in the rain."

Directly across the alley was a business apparently dedicated to offering coaches for hire. Adam grinned at him, amused at this eccentric character.

"Well, I don't suppose I *really* invented a new way," Mr. Folger said. "Perhaps I should share the credit with the great Greek mathematician Archimedes, who once said, 'The shortest distance between two points is a straight line.' And that's just what we've done."

"Thank you for your help, Mr. Folger. If I'm back in Boston sometime, I hope I can come by and see what you're up to. I'm no scientist, but I'd like to hear about what you're doing."

Mr. Folger reached out to shake Adam's hand. "I'd like that very much."

Adam quickly darted out of the door and across the alleyway and under the one open set of bay doors, where he found a man who told him he could arrange a ride for him as soon as one of his coaches came back. He had three out in town on rotation, but as long as they didn't pick up new hires, they'd be back to the stables shortly.

Sure enough, within about ten minutes a carriage pulled into the stable, and the man Adam had spoken to—whom he guessed was the proprietor, or at least the head man—and the driver both quickly worked to unhitch the horse that had just been out in the rainy cold and hitch up another horse, which had been patiently waiting his turn about the town.

Soon Adam was on his way to Beacon Hill.

IT ONLY TOOK ABOUT FIFTEEN minutes for them to arrive at the cross streets where Mr. Folger had told Adam he'd find the Wallace home. All of the homes in this area were brick. And they were all very large, just as Mr. Folger had noted in his journal. But which one belonged to the Wallace family?

Adam asked the driver if he knew. The driver gave a nod and pointed to one of the houses with a large iron gate out front.

"That's the one right there," he said.

"Thank you," Adam said. He paid the driver and then quickly ran over to the gate, trying his best to keep the rain off his head. Fortunately, the front gate wasn't locked, so he was able to go right up to the front door, where he looked for a cord to ring the bell, but there wasn't one. He grabbed the heavy door knocker and gave it a couple of loud thumps.

Soon he heard footsteps in the house coming towards the door.

"Be right there!" called out a familiar voice from inside.

Adam was relieved to have found the right place.

When the door swung open, there was Will Martin, completely astonished to see who was standing before him.

"Good Lord!" Will exclaimed. "Adam Fletcher! Is it really you?"

Adam nodded. "It is me. I am here." He looked up. "In the rain, in Boston, if you can believe it."

Will laughed. "Good heavens, come inside!" He motioned for Adam to follow him, then heartily shook his hand.

"What on earth has brought you all the way to Boston? Are you here alone? Please make yourself comfortable. Take off your coat and hat."

Adam did as Will suggested. He shook his head. "No, I'm actually not here alone. In fact, you'll never believe it, but I'm here with my father."

"Your father?" Will said. "Your father! You mean he's alive!?"

Adam nodded. "He is, and I was just as surprised as you are."

"Well, that's just wonderful to hear," said Will. "Did the two of you come here on business? Where is he?"

"He is trying to drum up some business in town right now, but we're not really here for that purpose. In fact, I've come with bad news, unfortunately."

"Oh." Will's expression changed to one of concern. "Well, come let's sit down in the library. You can tell me what's going on there."

Adam followed Will into a room about the size of the Martins' dining room back in New Bern. It was lined with built-in oak shelves from floor to ceiling, filled with more books than Adam had ever seen in one place in his life. There was a cozy fire in the fireplace, and a nearby round table held a tea service, where Will had apparently just been enjoying a cup.

"Can I get you some tea?" Will asked.

Adam nodded. "Thank you, that would be good."

As Will prepared a cup of tea for Adam, he encouraged him to have a seat.

"Tell me about this news," he said.

"It's Annabelle. A family from Edenton has taken her and is claiming she belongs to them. They're trying to say that she's one of their slaves who's run away."

"What?" Will twisted up his face in anger. "Annabelle's never even been a slave!" He handed Adam a cup of tea and then sat in the other chair at the table. "What about Charles Jr.?"

"He's fine. Well, he's as well as you might expect, given the circumstances. I mean, he's sick to death with worry over his wife, but otherwise he's fine. He's just anxious for you to come back. You see, a lawyer in Edenton said it will be necessary for you to come make a complaint, since Charles Jr. can make no complaint against a white man."

Will sighed, then shook his head in disbelief. "What kind of nonsense is this?"

"That's why I'm here, Will," said Adam. "Charles Jr. is counting on you to come straighten things out."

"Of course. Where is he? He didn't come with you?"

"No. We gave the lawyer in Edenton money for his food and lodging so he could stay close by and keep an eye on things with Annabelle. He knows we've come to get you. We hated to have to pull you away from your family, especially since you'd planned to be here through the winter, but maybe if you go back home and take care of this, you can get right back before the bitter cold sets in… not that I can imagine how it would get much colder than this."

"Oh, I'm not worried about coming back if I go down there. I want to get this all sorted out. But tell me everything you know about the situation. How in the world could this have happened?"

"There's a family by the name of Sanger. They live just outside of Edenton. I don't know that I'd go so far as to call it a plantation, but it's certainly a modest-sized farm. There appears to be one main house; it's not very big, and there are a handful of slaves from what we've seen."

"I see."

"And there's an overseer named Byrd. He's a horrible man."

Adam began to recount everything that had happened, from his grandfather sending him to New Bern to deliver that letter, to finding Charles Jr. in that pitiful state, to tracking down Billy Byrd and the Sangers and, by extension, Annabelle.

Will was pensive. He leaned back in the leather upholstered chair and nodded his head as he listened.

When Adam was done explaining everything, Will shook his head in dismay and clapped his hands to his knees. "Well, that's it, then, isn't it? We need to leave right away, then, don't we?"

"How quickly can you be ready?"

"Hmm." Will looked like he was thinking for a second. "It shouldn't take me long, but we'll need to give the women time to get their things together."

"You don't mean you're planning to bring the whole family back with you?" Adam said.

Will shook his head. "Well, no. I think I'll leave Catherine and Little Will here with her family. I can come back for them as soon as I'm able, but I do think I'll bring my sister back with us. She can also serve as a character witness to identify Annabelle in case there is any trouble."

Adam worried about how his father would react to him bringing Laney back with them, if he would even allow it. "You don't think your word will be sufficient?" he asked.

"It should be," said Will, "but no need to risk it. Anyway, she'll want to come with us. She's not happy here. For that matter, I'm not sure Laney is a good influence on these prim and proper Boston ladies. You know what a spirited girl she can be. I think these ladies aren't accustomed to a young woman who is so opinionated."

"Will, now listen," said Adam. "You know me. You know I'd love nothing more than to carry Miss Laney right back to North Carolina with us, but I think you should understand that we came here on my father's ship. It's definitely not some large, fancy vessel like the one that probably brought you here. It's just a sloop, a lot like Emmanuel's, but they run a tight ship, no foolishness."

"And?" Will said.

"You don't think she'll feel uncomfortable being the only woman on the ship for the week or more that it might take us to get back to North Carolina?"

Will furrowed his brow and nodded his head for a moment as he appeared to consider what Adam had said. "You raise a fair point," he responded, "but truthfully, my sister is uncomfortable here in Boston. She's uncomfortable with the city. And she hates the cold. She'll most likely be glad to trade a week of less-than-desirable accommodations for a ride back home. Anyway, we'd be bringing Aunt Celie with us. Laney wouldn't leave without her, so she won't be the only woman on board."

Good Lord, what is my father going to say? Adam could not imagine how this would go well.

Will glanced over at the heavy and excessively ornate golden clock across the room. It was almost ten.

"Maybe we should ask your sister. She really may not even want to go. Where is she?"

"I expect she should be back anytime now. They went to the market to buy groceries. Of course, they might've been distracted at the shops. The women left more than an hour ago, but the baby is in the nursery with Mrs. Tompkins, the nanny."

"In this horrible weather?" Adam asked.

"Catherine's used to it. She grew up with it. Nevertheless, she'll have to be back soon, since little William will be ready to eat and I won't be much help there."

"No, I don't guess you will," Adam said, chuckling.

Adam was a little bit surprised to hear that Laney hadn't taken to Boston. For selfish reasons, he was very pleased with the idea of her traveling back to North Carolina with them— that is, if his father would allow it. He'd had dreams since she'd been away—nightmares, really—that she'd been attending balls and dancing with other suitors there in Boston. One dream even forced him to imagine her dancing with one of his past rivals, Francis Smythe. Adam and Laney had no agreement between them. After all, he still had over a year before he'd finish his apprenticeship, and as an apprentice, he was forbidden to marry. Even if it weren't a contractual issue, he thought it would be ridiculous to make a proposal to her about the future until he was free of that, or at least until that was closer to the end of his term. Nevertheless, he got a lump in his throat whenever he thought about her being with someone else.

"Well, I suppose if we're going to be sailing home today, we might as well eat some decent food while we still have a chance. How about if I have the servants bring us some hors d'oeuvres?"

"Some what?" Adam asked.

Will rang a little bell, and a manservant appeared at the door. "You rang, Mr. Martin?"

"Yes, Edward. Would you mind bringing me and my friend a tray of hors d'oeuvres that we can eat while we wait on my wife and sister to return?"

Edward nodded and disappeared to handle his assigned task. Soon the servants of Catherine's family were shuffling in and out bringing trays of fancy-looking cookies, crackers, and cheeses, as well as a fresh, hot tea service.

Adam was glad to sample everything offered to him, especially since this might be the last normal food he'd eat for the next week. Nearly everything they ate at sea was salted to death, as a preservative.

He was grateful for the hospitality, but he was impatient for Laney to arrive. He hadn't seen her for months. It occurred to him that even though he was at Catherine's family's home, he hadn't met anyone from Catherine's family.

"Will," Adam said, "I heard that Catherine's father passed away and that her mother remarried a man named Wallace."

Will nodded. "Yes, in fact we only found out about her father's passing when we arrived. Evidently, he passed around the same time that our letter arrived saying that Catherine was expecting a child. Her mother didn't want to throw sadness in with the joy of Catherine's news, so she opted to keep it a secret until we came to visit."

"Did Catherine take the news well?" asked Adam.

"Not really," said Will. "She was actually quite upset, but she is so gracious. She understood that her mother was just trying to look out for her."

"I reckon she was also surprised her mother had already remarried," Adam said.

"A bit, yes, but Neill—that's his name—is a good man. He's a big, tall fellow, and he's loud, but by all accounts he has a heart of gold. Actually, he and Catherine's mother have gone down to Plymouth for a couple of days to visit a Presbyterian minister from Neill's old home territory."

"Presbyterian, huh? Interesting." Adam really didn't know what that meant, theologically speaking, other than that the Presbyterians were a little bit different than the Church of England back in Beaufort. "What business is he in?"

"Neill? He owns a veritable fleet of ships, but he doesn't get involved in the details of the business. He has merchants here in America and in Scotland handling the business on his behalf. He spends most of his time on philanthropic pursuits."

Adam was impressed at that. He regretted that he wouldn't have a chance to meet him before leaving Boston. He sounded like someone his grandfather would definitely like to know.

AFTER ADAM AND WILL HAD spent a few more minutes catching up, a familiar woman's voice could be heard in the foyer. "It's highway robbery what they charge! That's what it is!"

Adam smiled. "I reckon that's Miss Laney."

Will raised his eyebrow and cocked his head to the side in mild embarrassment. "I'm afraid it is. Let's go see them."

Adam started to follow Will out of the room and down the hall towards the parlor, where Laney was still railing about something as one of the family's servants helped her, Catherine, and Aunt Celie remove their wet coats and hats.

Will motioned for him to wait in an alcove by the servant's stairs so he could surprise her. Adam could easily see what was happening in the foyer, but he wouldn't be spotted from where he was standing.

"Laney," said Will as he entered the room, "you might lower your voice a bit. Little William is sleeping soundly, but he won't be for long if you keep carrying on like this."

Aunt Celie excused herself from the room. Adam assumed she probably had gone right away to check on the baby.

Laney rolled her eyes at her brother. "Sorry!" she whispered.

Catherine shook her head and smiled at her husband as she held out one of her market baskets for him to help himself to whatever was inside. Will lifted the tea towel covering the basket and took out an apple.

"No wonder so many of the people here look sad all the time!" Laney exclaimed. "Who can save money when purchasing ordinary food costs such an exorbitant amount of money? For goodness' sake! How do they get by in this city without more gardens? But then, how could they have decent gardens with so much nasty weather?"

Catherine crossed the room to take the baskets she was holding into the dining room. She left them there and returned to the foyer, where she spoke to her husband. "I'll go check on little William. Has he been fussy?"

Will shook his head. "No, good as gold."

Without missing a beat, Laney resumed her diatribe, albeit in a loud whisper directed at her brother, since Catherine had left the room. "Honestly! It's an absolute wonder we're not completely overrun in the South, given the crowding and weather up here! How do these people stand to stay here?"

"You want to go home, Laney?" Will asked with a smile. "Is that it?"

"Oh, if I had a way, I'd be on the first boat back *this afternoon*!"

"Even in this rain and cold?" Will asked with a skeptical look on his face.

"Yes, even in this rain," Laney said with a huff.

Adam could see that Will struggled to keep from laughing.

Will said, "Well, maybe we can arrange something."

Laney rolled her eyes and was about to go up the main staircase when Will motioned for Adam to come out of the alcove.

"Go on and get packed, girl, and I'll take you back," Adam said as he came around the corner.

Laney's eyes grew enormous and she darted towards him like she was about to hug him, but she looked at her brother, then stopped just short of it.

"What on earth!? How did you get here? When did you get here?!"

Adam gave her a half smile. "Well, I wish I could tell you I'm here just to take you home, but in truth I'm not here with happy news."

Laney furrowed her brow and looked quickly from Adam

to her brother. She was evidently able to see the look of concern on both of their faces.

"What's all this about?"

Will took a deep breath before answering in a quiet voice. Adam assumed Will didn't want Aunt Celie to hear the news from down the hall. "It's Annabelle. It's a long story, but she's being held as a slave on a farm near Edenton. We have to go back to sort things out."

Laney was visibly shaken. "What? Edenton? How in the world?"

"We'll have plenty of time to explain everything on *La Dama*," said Adam, "but for now, if you do want to come, maybe you ought to just go on and get your things packed."

"*La Dama*?" Laney exclaimed. "Your father's ship?"

Adam nodded.

"What?"

"Go on and get ready, and we'll have plenty of time to talk about everything."

Without wasting a single second, Laney turned and ran up the stairs and down the hall to get her things together.

Will told Adam to go have a seat and wait for him in the library while he got his things together and explained to his wife what was happening.

Fortunately, a little more than an hour later it had finally stopped raining. The Wells family servants helped load up Laney's old trunk, hatbox, and another new trunk—apparently to hold all of the things she'd bought since she'd been in Boston—on their carriage, along with Will's one small trunk and another new, small trunk belonging to Aunt Celie.

Unfortunately, Catherine's mother and stepfather didn't return before her family left. After the departing Martin family members said their goodbyes to Catherine, baby William, and Mrs. Wells, they were on their way to the harbor to board *La Dama*.

Of the members of the Martin family traveling in the carriage with Adam, Aunt Celie was the only one who looked visibly shaken, and understandably so. She silently wept, her face turned fixedly towards the window, watching the city pass them by. Laney held on to her hand in an effort to comfort her.

Adam felt sympathy for the woman but was at a loss as to what to say or do given the circumstances. He knew how she had worried about her son being granted his freedom, and she didn't seem particularly fond of Annabelle in the first place. He also knew, however, that her son's freedom had nothing whatsoever to do with what had happened to Annabelle, nor did it have anything to do with the situation in which her son and his wife now found themselves.

He wondered if Aunt Celie was imagining him in danger and if she was, by extension, blaming Annabelle for it. He tried to push the thoughts out of his head of what might be happening with the pair left back in Edenton. Whatever sprang to his mind was never good. There was nothing he could do about it in the short term, so it seemed like an exercise in futility to dwell on it.

Chapter Fifteen

ONCE THEY ARRIVED AT THE dock where La Dama was moored, Adam was relieved to see his father standing down by the sloop talking to one of his crew members. He quickly excused himself from the carriage while Will and the driver unloaded the luggage. He wanted a chance to talk to his father about the women traveling with them.

"Absolutely not," Santiago said, seemingly astonished that his son would even request such a thing.

"You don't understand," said Adam. "It was Will's idea. Laney hates it here, and Will is insistent she travel back with us. And if she's coming, Aunt Celie is coming too. Laney never likes to travel anywhere without her if she can help it."

"Aunt Celie?"

"Charles Jr.'s mother, remember?"

"Adam, maybe you forgot our conversation about the precarious situation I presently have with my crew. And furthermore, I do not know if you have noticed, but I have a ship here full of men. They are not gentlemen. They are *marineros*. Never in the entire time I have commanded this vessel have we ever traveled with a woman on board."

"What about my mother? She says you and her were married on *La Dama*."

Santiago laughed. "We had a wedding, yes! Traveling, no! Where do you think we are going to put a young lady like Miss Martin—and her servant, no less!—for a voyage that will take a week or more? In the steerage?" He laughed. "Certainly not in the *castillo de proa* with the crew."

Adam narrowed his eyes and said matter-of-factly, "Of course not! I had hoped you might be a gentleman and give up your quarters for the women."

Santiago put his hand on his hip and sighed, then looked off to the side and shook his head, clearly angered. He turned his focus back to Adam. "I know how to be a gentleman and I do not need my son to tell me anything about it. I am enough of a gentleman to know this vessel is no place for a lady."

"And yet you call her *La Dama*."

Just then Will came walking towards them on the dock, with Laney and Aunt Celie following close behind.

"Everything alright here?" he asked.

Adam nodded. "Yes, I was just talking to my father about him offering his quarters to the ladies. By the way, let me introduce you."

Santiago smiled awkwardly. He reached out his hand to shake Will's, then said, "We have met a long time ago, before he moved to New Bern."

Will nodded. "Indeed we have. You remember?" He gave Santiago a broad smile. "Listen, we really don't want to put you out, but I think it's best if we take my sister back with us. She's miserable here, and Aunt Celie will be a wreck worrying about her son. I'll gladly pay you for their passage."

Santiago cut his eyes at Adam before he turned back to

Will. "No, that will not be necessary. It is my pleasure to take you all back. We do not want to leave your sister behind, or her *sirvienta*."

Adam knew his father would give him grief over this, but he didn't care. There was no time to argue about the situation, nor did Adam have any inclination to do so.

Santiago gave a couple of members of his crew orders in Spanish. Adam assumed he'd instructed them to go fetch all of the Martins' luggage.

Once everyone was on board, Laney and Aunt Celie were shown to the officer's cabin, where they would be staying during the voyage. Inside there was a small table and a bunk on either side of the cabin. Each bunk had a curtain, for privacy. Beneath the stern lights along the aft area was a long bench for storage.

"We'll let you two ladies get settled here," said Adam. "We'll be back shortly."

He then helped Will take his trunk down below deck to the ship's hold, where he noticed some unfamiliar cargo. His father must've lined up some business in Boston, after all, he thought. He then showed Will the area in steerage where he could sleep. Once Will was familiar with his accommodations, the two men returned above deck to check on the ladies before they cast off. Adam looked over at Laney, but Aunt Celie caught his eye. She was standing close to Laney, tightly clutching her handkerchief. Adam suddenly remembered Aunt Celie's insistence in the past that they pray before traveling. He didn't have to think much about it when his grandfather's ship set sail, as Emmanuel always had the reverend come say a word before his crew left, but it was obviously not a habit his father or his crew had in place for *La Dama*.

He leaned over and discreetly asked his father if he might say a word before they left port.

Santiago gave him a surprised look and rolled his eyes, but then he shrugged and nodded. "Of course. It is probably a wise idea, especially with these visitors on board."

He called out to his crew in Spanish and told them something that made them stand at attention. He then held his hand out to Adam to indicate that he could go ahead and pray.

Adam looked across the deck at Aunt Celie and Laney and smiled. He motioned for them to step out of the cabin for a moment, and then he bowed his head and spoke aloud. "Heavenly Father, please grant us swift and safe travels back to North Carolina. Help us protect the guests traveling with us and keep them safe from storms and other dangers at sea. We thank you for your watchful eye and for blessing us with tolerable weather for the journey home. We ask these things in the name of our Lord and Savior, Jesus Christ. Amen."

"Amen," said Santiago, crossing himself. He then called out more instructions to his crew and they cast off.

Adam could see Aunt Celie hold Laney's hand, and she gave it a squeeze. She smiled at him in gratitude, but he could tell she was fighting tears as best as she could.

In warmer climes, everyone would happily be on deck as they left port, but the frigid wind cut like a saber through anyone unfortunate enough to be exposed to it. Adam accompanied Will, Laney, and Aunt Celie back into the officer's cabin.

He explained to the ladies that they could take a few necessities out of their trunks, but then it would all have to be taken down below.

"But what about that big bench over there?" Laney asked.

"That's where my father and the mate keep their things."

Laney seemed nervous about parting with her luggage, but she complied willingly.

"We'll let you ladies rest here, but can we bring you anything? Or answer any questions?" Adam asked.

"Where the kitchen?" asked Aunt Celie.

Will put his hand on her back. "Oh, there's not a regular kitchen on this ship. The men have a sort of kitchen below deck, but there's no proper kitchen as you've been accustomed to using."

"Well, I can help with the cookin if y'all just show me where to go."

"Please, Aunt Celie," said Adam. "You're a guest on *La Dama*. Leave the cooking to Tony. That's what he's here for."

Aunt Celie looked skeptical, but she nodded in understanding. She leaned forward and sort of whispered, as if she was afraid Santiago or someone in his crew might hear her, "What kind of things they cook, these Spaniards?"

Laney raised her eyebrows, indicating that she'd been wondering the same thing.

"A lot of beans and rice and pork. Sometimes beef if they have it," Adam responded. "Don't worry. I think you'll like it. After all, if a cook is no good, they can always just throw him overboard."

Aunt Celie gave a little laugh and shook her head at Adam. "Oh! Mr. Adam! You know better than that!"

Adam and Will chuckled and left the ladies to rest in the cabin.

When they came out on deck, Santiago, who had apparently just finished discussing some business with the boatswain, said, "Adam, I need to have a word with you, please."

Will said, "I'll go on down below and get to my paperwork. There's a lot to do."

"Fine," said Adam. "I'll be down in a bit to get you so you can help me bring down the ladies' things."

Once Will had gone below deck, Santiago pulled his son aside.

"*Mijo*, I do not know if you understand this, but I *am* going to be staying in my cabin. You will need to let Will know about this."

Adam gave his father a confused look. "There are only two bunks in there."

His father looked irritated. "*Ya se*. Which is why I did not want women on board. Nevertheless, that is where I will be staying. I have just asked Rafa to convert the aft storage bench beneath the stern lights to a bunk for me to sleep, and he will add some little doors on the bunks to give them their privacy — which will perhaps make them feel more secure than the *cortinas*."

"And Beto?" Adam asked. "I had assumed you both might stay in steerage with Will."

"Beto can stay in steerage, but I will maintain my position on this sloop. It is bad for the discipline of this vessel for me to do anything else."

Adam wasn't sure how he was going to explain all of this to Will, or what Will would say, much less what Laney and Aunt Celie would think about it, but it didn't really matter. That was the way it would have to be.

Santiago told Adam to go and inform Will of the situation and that he would explain more later.

Adam went back below deck to find Will sitting on a crate writing in a leather-bound ledger.

"What are you working on?" he asked him.

"Oh, I'm just writing some notes down regarding the situation with Annabelle and Charles Jr. I'm making a list of the various charges I plan to make as soon as we reach Edenton, as well as what we'll need to prove that Annabelle and Charles Jr. are who we claim they are."

"Will," said Adam. "You know how I was just talking to my father?"

Will nodded. "Yes. Of course." Adam could tell Will sensed he was about to tell him something difficult.

"It turns out we have a challenging situation on this ship."

"What's that?"

"My father wasn't expecting any passengers other than you. It's my fault, but I took him by surprise by asking if Laney and Aunt Celie could come with us, but he graciously is allowing it."

Will put down his pencil and crossed his hands in front of him. "I know. And I'm very grateful for that. I told him I'd be happy to pay him for their passage."

"I know," said Adam. "He's not worried about that. The issue is the crew. Most of the men on this ship are new crew members, and they already are grumbling about this unexpected trip to Boston. It's imperative that he maintains order on this vessel, but he's afraid he can't do that if he's kicked out of his own cabin."

Will wrinkled his brow. He obviously didn't understand exactly what Adam was getting at.

"Will, my father is going to be staying in the cabin with your sister and Aunt Celie."

"What!? That's completely inappropriate!"

"He's having Rafael, the ship's carpenter, prepare him a bunk at the back of the cabin, and there will be doors installed on the women's bunks, but for the benefit of discipline on the ship, he needs to stay in his place. The ship's mate will be staying here in steerage with you, though."

"I don't have to tell you, Adam, that I don't like the sound of this at all."

Adam shrugged. "Well, neither do I, and frankly, my father's not happy about it either, but it's the way things are going to have to be. You have to know you have nothing to worry about, though."

"The look of it!" Will exclaimed. "And my sister won't like this one bit."

"I don't doubt it," said Adam, "but I'll leave you to discuss that with her. And you can talk to my father about it later. Maybe he can explain more. I'll get another one of the men to help me bring their luggage down here. You just go ahead with your work."

Adam decided he should probably go find his father and at least try to make peace. It would be a miserable voyage with his father angry at him the whole way.

ADAM WAS ABLE TO GET Paco to help him bring the women's luggage down below deck. He was amused to see the number of things that Laney felt necessary to remove from her luggage, but she insisted on having the little pile she had made on her bunk, and in fact, insisted that she would keep it all in the bed with her at night, if necessary.

When Adam completed that task, he found his father talking to Beto near the helm.

He knew it would be out of order for him to interrupt them, but nevertheless he needed to talk to him as his father right now, not as his captain. He just stood there watching the two of them talking in Spanish while waiting for his father to acknowledge him.

Finally, Santiago said something to Beto, indicating he needed to have a word with his son.

They walked over and stood by a more or less secluded spot along the port rail.

"Goodness gracious," Adam said. "Why does he look so mad all the time?"

"I do not think he is mad. I think he is very serious about his job, and he is very good at it."

Adam shrugged. "Maybe so. But still, he doesn't seem to enjoy it very much."

Santiago studied his son for a moment. "*Mijo*, you wanted to talk to me about something?"

"Yes. Yes, I did."

Santiago raised his eyebrows as if to say, *Well, get on with it.*

Adam said, "I know all of this was unexpected, but I don't understand why you're so upset."

His father looked down and shook his head in disbelief. "Ah, *mijo*, you are a man, and yet you are still just like a child in many ways."

"What does that even mean? How am I being childish?"

Santiago was slow to respond. He appeared to be thinking long and hard about how he wanted to answer his son.

Finally, he said, "Do you not think it would have been

wise to discuss this with me about bring *dos mujeres* on board? And one of them *una negra*! And just to push me even further, you expected me to offer my own cabin to these women and abandon my place?"

"Would you rather they be in steerage?"

"No! I would not have brought them in the first place."

"Then why did you go along with it?" Adam asked, although he braced himself, fully expecting his father to come down hard on him for even asking. He knew he really hadn't given him much of a choice.

"Like you say, I am a gentleman. I am enough of a gentleman to know that women do not belong on *this ship*. There are many problems here."

"I can tell that you think so, but beyond you having to give up your cabin, I'm not really sure what problems you're talking about. Seems like you run a tight ship, and the men are getting the work done."

"Well, let us think about it, shall we?" Santiago's tone was biting. "Aside from the fact that I am inconvenienced even by coming here to Boston to help your friends with this problem, you have brought my authority into question in front of my men. And as if that were not bad enough, do you have any idea what is down in the hold of this vessel right now?"

"Wait, wait, wait," Adam said. "How have I brought your authority into question?"

"*¡Ay Dios! ¡Ayudeme, por favor!*" Santiago was clearly exasperated. "I do not know if you realize this or not, *mijo*, but I was raised in a very different place than you, with very different values. The men in *this* crew will not understand, nor will they appreciate, their *capitán* bringing into the officer's cabin a young Englishwoman and her *sirviente* and displacing the mate. I can assure you they do not think about women the way you, or even I, might think of them. *Además*, they do not like the English very much. Nevertheless, they would not see a problem if I am taking only Will or even another Englishman on board, because he is a man and it is business. Women have no business here. This crew will be thinking this is not a passenger ship and it never has been a passenger ship. It is not our job to transport women here and there simply because they want to come along."

Adam started to speak, but before he could even get a word out, his father continued.

"Do you speak Spanish, *mijo*? No, you do not. I will tell you something that I would have preferred not to discuss, but now you will know."

Adam took a deep breath, then crossed his arms to show he was paying attention.

His father began to explain. "We have a very serious problem. There are some men in my crew right now who I am told are making trouble. They are upset about sailing to Boston on an unscheduled *viaje*, and I am hearing that they are complaining about it. They did not know when they agreed to leave Cuba that they would right away have to do something like this. I will likely dismiss them from my crew when we return because they are insubordinate, but for now I need them to help us get back to Carolina." Santiago leaned in towards Adam and whispered, furiously pointing his finger downward to emphasize his point, "But if they feel they have been pushed too far, there are very real dangers. Do you understand?"

Adam nodded.

"Do you think I want women on board if the situation turns violent?"

"Of course not."

"What was it about the cargo? Is there a problem with what's in the hold?"

Santiago laughed in frustration. "Is there a problem with what is in the hold? Ha! Do you know what is in the hold?"

Of course Adam didn't. He said nothing but raised his eyebrows to indicate he was waiting to find out.

"I was able to talk with a man who runs some whalers from this colony. I purchased a great quantity of whale oil from him along with other *productos de ballena*."

"Bye-yaena?"

"*Ballena* is 'whale.' I know where I can sell these things and make a good profit, but there are two difficulties: first, this oil is only supposed to be sold to buyers in Britain, so again, we are *contrabandistas*; and second, every member of this crew also knows the value of what is on board and it could make any of them rich men. I would like very much to avoid mutiny, but I fear the temptation will be ever present."

"Alright," said Adam. "I'm sorry. Just let me know if there's anything I can do to help keep things in order until we get back home."

"Just keep your eyes and ears open," Santiago said, "and do not give any of the officers a reason to complain about *you*."

"Yes, sir."

Since his watch wouldn't be for a few hours yet, Adam decided to go rest in his bunk and maybe write a little bit in his journal.

ADAM MUST'VE BEEN MORE TIRED than he realized. When he climbed in his bunk, he ended up not writing in his journal at all. Instead, he lay down with his fingers intertwined behind his head, knees up, and he started thinking about all that his father had told him. He went through a mental list of the men in the crew, and he tried to figure out which of them might be causing problems. Evidently, he thought so hard it sent him right off to sleep.

He was awakened by being tossed hard against the side of his bunk. He immediately realized they'd found their way into another a storm. Probably the same one they'd left in Boston. One glance over towards the hatch verified the fact, as water was starting to pour in. He must've been sleeping very hard to have not felt the violent rocking of the ship before now.

He quickly put on his boots and tarred canvas coat and climbed up the ladder with the other sailors, who had also been awakened from rest. It was a slippery task, as icy rain pounded the ship as they made their ascent.

As soon as he cleared the hatch, he looked across the deck and saw the face of a terrified Laney peering out of one of the scuttles of the cabin. He took for granted sailing through storms, but he doubted Laney or Aunt Celie had ever gone through anything like this before. He ran over and gave them a sympathetic expression, then he pulled the wooden covers down over both of the tiny windows, which would hopefully keep out most of the rain and help them feel more secure.

Everyone in the crew was frantically working to keep the ship afloat. Men struggled to maintain their footing as they sloshed around the deck to lash down the guns and anything else that wasn't already fastened in place, while others worked quickly to furl the sails. The tarps that ordinarily covered the hatches were no match for the crashing waves, and a couple of men desperately tried to keep the bilge pumped so the ship wouldn't take on too much water as it was tossed to and fro in the waves.

This was the worst storm Adam had ever sailed through, and he prayed they'd make it out alive. He could only imagine the state of panic that Laney and Aunt Celie were in with the intense winds, booming cracks of thunder, and distant lightning, the ocean spilling over onto the deck, and the gigantic waves causing the sloop to pitch and roll violently.

He also remembered Will was in the steerage. He only hoped his friend had the good sense to grab on to a pole or something else that was fixed in place.

Chapter Sixteen

WHEN THEY FINALLY MADE IT through the storm, the entire crew seemed to let out a huge, collective sigh of relief.

Adam was able to get permission to check on Laney and Aunt Celie. Both women were soaking wet from the water that had mercilessly poured into the cabin. The two had apparently climbed together into one of the bunks, where they were sitting with their backs against the hull, huddled together, holding on to one another for dear life and still praying when Adam found them.

After making sure neither of them were hurt and assuring them that the ordeal was over, he excused himself from the cabin and told them that his father was busy on deck so they could feel safe to change into dry clothes—that was, if they could find any. He wanted to go down now and check on Will.

When he made it below deck to the steerage compartment, Will looked as white as a sheet. He had been able to lash himself to something, but that did nothing to prevent him from vomiting throughout the ordeal, evident by the mess that was beneath their feet.

"You going to be alright?" Adam asked him.

Will nodded. He still looked like he felt very sick.

"Don't worry," Adam said. "I think we're past the storms. Lord willing, it'll be calm seas from here on out—or at least calmer than what we've just been through."

Adam knew that there was no way he could guarantee they'd have calm seas the rest of the way, but looking at Will, he could tell his friend needed some words of comfort.

"Adam," Will said to him just before he was about to ascend the ladder back up to the main deck, "I need to tell you something."

"What's that?"

"I was hesitant to even mention it, but shortly before the storm became very violent, there were two men down here and I overheard them talking in Spanish, and I think there's something you should know."

"Do you speak Spanish?" Adam asked, surprised.

"Oh, unfortunately no, but I did learn Latin, and there are some similarities here and there between the two languages."

"What is it? What did you hear?"

"I may be wrong about this—but I don't think so, but after all of this—I just can't *not* tell you, in case there's something to it."

"Goodness gracious, Will, what in the world is it?"

"It sounded like something, something—I think it was *esta noche superemos el patrón.*"

Adam looked confused. "I have no idea what that means."

"In Latin, to say *superemus* means something like 'let's overtake' or 'let's overcome,' and *patron* can mean a lot of things, but in this context I think it probably means 'the captain'—your father. That word *noche* sounds like the Latin word for 'night,' so they may be planning to do something tonight."

Adam immediately realized what Will was suggesting. He wouldn't have been as concerned if it weren't for everything his father had told them when they first left Boston.

"Who were they? I mean, what did they look like?"

When Will told him who they were, Adam couldn't believe that either of them would be involved.

"I need to go let my father know about this," Adam said. "Keep your eyes and ears open and let me know if you see or hear anything else."

"Oh, most definitely," said Will.

WHEN ADAM WAS BACK ON deck, he intended to go right to his father about what he'd learned, but unfortunately he was immediately reprimanded by the boatswain, Ernesto, for being late for his watch. Adam would've had no idea what he was being upbraided for, except his father chastised him when he heard what Ernesto said.

How am I going to get my father alone to tell him about this? One of the men whom Will had just described *was* Ernesto. The other was the ship's second mate, Miguel.

He decided this was no time to worry about protocol, and instead he ignored the boatswain and leaned over and whispered in his father's ear.

Santiago looked at him. "What? Just get to work!"

Evidently, Adam's face told him something was very wrong.

His father ended up saying a few words to Ernesto and then pulled Adam over to the other side of the ship.

"What is it?"

"I just heard something from Will that I think you need to know."

"What? And this better be important, because you are already late for your watch."

Adam nodded. "I know. And it is. Will said just before the storm turned violent he overheard two of the men down below talking in Spanish, but because he understands Latin, and there are some similar words, he was alarmed by what they said."

"What did they say?" Santiago looked concerned.

"I hope I get this right," Adam said. "They said something like *Esta noche superemos el patrón.*"

His father's face fell. "I understand exactly what this means."

"Are they planning a mutiny?"

"Someone is. Who said this?"

Adam took a deep breath and then exhaled sharply before he answered. "It sounds like it was Miguel and Ernesto."

Santiago clenched his fist and looked stunned. "*¡Ay, Dios mio!* How can this be? Miguel and his brother, Beto, have been with me since they started sailing." He was pensive and stroked the short black beard on his chin. "*Esta es una situación muy delicada.* We need to be sure that this is true before we do anything. If Will is wrong, or if you are wrong, then it will be a very big mistake for me to accuse my men of something when they are innocent."

"What can we do?" Adam said.

"I suspect I may know what is happening. Rafa told me

he was not able to find some of his tools when he went in the cabin to convert the bench to a bed for me."

"You think some of the men are stealing his tools?"

"They could be. Maybe some of the men have been hiding the tools somewhere on board, because I can tell you this, two men are not going to stage a mutiny by themselves. If it is being planned, there are more involved."

Adam thought for a moment back to the items he'd noticed out of place on the ship when something dawned on him.

"I know it is my watch, but I need to go check someplace. I think I may know where they're hiding things."

Santiago motioned for him to go.

Adam went down into the forecastle, where there was a small opening in the bulkhead that led to where the anchor cable was stored. It was on the deck of the forecastle near right there that he had found a carpenter's adze—completely out of place—just as he was about to go up top during the storm. He reached around in the cable tier and, just as he suspected, several missing items had been stashed in there. He didn't want to pull them out and let on that he knew what was happening until he had a chance to tell his father.

He hurried back on deck to let him know what he had found.

Once his father found this out, he directed Ernesto to sound his whistle to get all hands on deck. Soon every member of the crew was there before them, impatiently waiting to find out what they'd been called up there for.

Santiago started speaking to his crew very loudly and sternly—in Spanish, of course. Adam watched the men's reactions to try to ascertain what was being said. It was remarkable, because at one point during his father's speech it became clear to him who was in on this mutiny, as the guilty deckhands were all looking at each other nervously. Of course Adam already knew about the guilty officers. He wondered how long it would be before one of them lashed out at the charges, and he was not disappointed, as the first one to run towards his father in a desperate attack was Joaquín, one of the deckhands, who always seemed to be talking about him when they were on watch together. No sooner had he launched his attack at the captain than the whole crew descended into a melee.

Adam welcomed the opportunity to tackle the other annoying deckhand, Nacho. He had wanted to punch him in the face since the first time they were on watch together, and he was glad to finally do it. They wrestled back and forth and got in punches wherever they could, but ultimately Adam was able to overpower his opponent and pin him down with his knee in Nacho's back. Apparently, Paco had seen what was happening with Adam and Nacho, so he came over and offered Adam assistance in binding his hands and feet with some extra line.

In spite of being outnumbered by one, those loyal to Santiago disabled all of the traitorous crew members by tying them up. Soon they were all bound and under close watch, as they would be for the rest of the voyage.

While Adam, his father, and Beto were all relieved to have discovered the plot before the traitors had a chance to execute it by surprise, they still had to contend with the fact that now they would be sailing with less than half the crew, and both the captain and mate would be required to do some tasks that they ordinarily would never be expected to do. Not to mention Beto had to finish out this voyage knowing his own brother had been in on the mutinous scheme.

They still had at least five days of sailing ahead of them before they got to Edenton, so it was decided—at his suggestion—that even Will would serve as a member of the crew. Adam knew his friend never thought law school would lead him on a path to becoming a sailor, but alas, a green hand he would be. Desperate times and all…

Chapter Seventeen

"Oh thank God," Adam said as the town of Edenton came into view. This was undoubtedly one of the longest weeks of his life. He was just glad to be back in North Carolina and finally able to go with Will to help free Annabelle.

Adam and his father had discussed the best course of action for when they arrived. It was decided that *La Dama* would dock just long enough to allow Adam, Will, Laney, and Aunt Celie to disembark and for their luggage to be taken off the ship. Santiago planned to continue sailing with his crew to Cuba so that he could dismiss the men who had caused all of the problems and then find a buyer for the whale products he procured in Boston.

The weather was not warm in Edenton, but it felt much more tolerable than the cold they had been dealing with in Boston. Adam suggested that Will, Laney, and Aunt Celie wait with their things by the dock while he went to find a coach to bring them to the house of Mr. King, the attorney. He headed straight for Mr. Vickers's house.

He could see the coach in front of the stable. He knocked

on the door and found the man who'd taken him and his father to Virginia. The portly driver looked pleased to see Adam, and he was happy to hitch one of his horses up to go fetch Will and the ladies, along with their luggage, and then he took them all straight to the home of Mr. King.

Will asked Mr. Vickers if he would wait out front with the ladies until he and Adam had a chance to announce their presence and see if it would be alright for them to bring the luggage inside. Adam had already told Will it might be a good idea rather than letting the women follow them right inside, on the off chance that there was some upsetting news regarding Annabelle.

What Adam did not expect, however, was what he learned from Mr. King when they were first escorted into his office.

After Will and Mr. King were introduced to one another, Adam was hit with the devastating news.

"Mr. Fletcher, I'm sorry to tell you this, but your man Charles Jr. took off not more than two days after you and your father left this place."

Adam made no effort to hide his shock, nor did Will.

"What?" Adam said. "He took off? What on earth happened? Why would you let him leave?"

"Calm down, young man," said Mr. King. "Did you expect me to keep him a prisoner here? You and your father did say he was a free man, didn't you?"

"Yes, but my question for you is this: Why would he have wanted to 'take off,' as you put it, in the first place? His wife is just a few miles from here. He *knew* we were on our way back with Will so he could help him get Annabelle back."

Mr. King smiled at Will as though he were a bit

embarrassed, then motioned for Will and Adam to both take a seat. He sat down in the chair behind his desk.

"I should think you would want to sit down for this. Not only has Charles Jr. taken off, but his wife is no longer at the Sanger farm, and the Sangers are claiming he came and stole her away. So now they're both wanted as fugitives, and there is a reward that's been posted for their capture: one amount for the safe return of Annabelle, whom they're calling Peg, and a slightly lesser amount for Charles Jr., dead or alive."

Adam and Will exchanged a worried look.

"They'd pay less of a reward for him and take him dead or alive why? Because he's a free man? So he's worth nothing to them." Adam dropped his head forward and rested his elbows on his knees. He took a deep breath, then huffed out the air in frustration. They had gone so far, made it back against all odds, and now this.

"If we can find them first," Will said, "Lord willing we can clear Charles Jr.'s name and secure Annabelle's safety."

Adam finally looked up. "I can't believe this. Honest to God, I cannot believe this." He shook his head to reiterate his disbelief.

"We have been through hell to make it back to Edenton as quickly as we possibly could. We nearly faced mutiny on board my father's sloop, and that was only because it wasn't enough that the weather tried to drown us all. Now we finally make it back to this place, and for what? Who knows where they will have taken off to? Charles Jr. is in a panic, and one thing we can be sure of—they won't be going back to your place in New Bern, Will. He'll know they'll look for them there first."

Will thought for a moment, then spoke. "I think we

need to make a visit out to the Sanger place, just so we can see for ourselves that neither Charles Jr. nor Annabelle are being held there. Then I can also let them know that I am here, who I am, and that I will own their farm and everything on it if anything happens to either of them." He looked over at Mr. King and said, "You know as well as I do that I don't have the power to take all that they have, but they are unlikely to know that."

Mr. King nodded and smiled. "Well, I like your strategy, anyway."

"What about your sister and Aunt Celie?" Adam said. "They're still out waiting in the coach."

"Good heavens!" Mr. King exclaimed. "Well, by all means bring them in."

"It's a good thing they weren't in here to hear all of this. Will and I will need to break this news to them gently."

Mr. King furrowed his brow in understanding. "Well," he said, "let's go on outside, and I'll call Pearson in here to help us bring in all of the luggage. How about if I go with you out to the Sangers' place, Mr. Martin, and you stay back here with the women, Mr. Fletcher?"

"That sounds like a reasonable plan," said Adam.

As soon as Will left, Adam sat down with Laney and Aunt Celie and explained to them what he had learned about Charles Jr. and Annabelle disappearing, and the rewards out for the two of them.

"Oh Lawd! Oh Lawd!" The distraught mother clung tightly to her handkerchief and Laney's hand, and her head dropped forward towards her lap as she dissolved into tears. "Oh Lawd, help me! Help me!"

Adam knew that Aunt Celie's cry wasn't just an emotional reaction or empty exclamation but a plea to God to help her have the strength to get through this circumstance.

Admittedly, in his heart he also prayed God would help them find Charles Jr. and Annabelle before any would-be bounty hunters or slave catchers did, but he feared they wouldn't.

Laney put her arm around Aunt Celie, and the old woman sobbed into her shoulder. She shook her head, and her brow was wrinkled with worry.

"Aunt Celie," Adam said. "Maybe you can help us, huh?"

Aunt Celie looked up, her eyes wet with tears. She dabbed them with her handkerchief.

"Listen, think real hard about this," Adam said. "We know they've probably not gone back to Will's place in New Bern. It would be too dangerous. Do y'all know anywhere else between here and there where they might try to find safety?"

Aunt Celie sniffed, then took a deep breath, punctuated by attempts to stifle sobs, before she answered. "As a matter of fact, I sure can think of where they might've gone to."

"Where?" Laney asked. "Where do you think they might've gone?"

"We ain't really s'posed to talk about this, but everybody prob'ly already knows, anyway. Annabelle's daddy is a white planter over in Pitt County. He sent the girl and her mother to live with friends in Craven County right after her mama had her and he saw that she was his child. He didn't wanna cause no problems with his wife."

"So you think they may have gone there?" Laney asked.

"If they can't go back to New Bern, that's the next place I think they'd go. I heard the man's wife is dead now, so she ain't around to be upset if her husband's mulatto daughter turns up."

"Alright," said Adam, "I think we need to go there to look for them, then. Lord willing they'll be there, and we can keep them safe until this whole business is resolved."

Laney said, "From what I've heard Will mention about cases related to stolen property and so forth—and that's what we're dealing with here, a claim that Charles Jr. stole Annabelle, who these people are calling their stolen 'property,' Peg—the only way for Charles Jr. to prove his innocence is to appear in court *and* for witnesses to testify that Annabelle is his wife in court and that she never was the property of these wicked people."

"That makes sense," said Adam. "I wonder if they'll have to appear in court here, or if it will be in New Bern."

Laney shrugged. "I'm not sure, but my brother will know."

It took a couple of hours for Will and Mr. King to return from going out to the Sanger farm. Will explained that he insisted upon seeing for himself whether or not Charles Jr. and Annabelle were being held at that farm, and he also said that he informed them he would be filing a suit against them as soon as he got back into town. Among other things, the chief complaint would be the Sangers's kidnapping one of his employees, Annabelle, under fraudulent pretenses.

Adam asked Will about what Laney had said as far as whether or not Charles Jr. and Annabelle would have to appear in court and where. Will said at the very least Charles Jr. would need to, and it would need to be in Edenton.

Adam then proceeded to explain to Will what Aunt Celie

had said about Annabelle's father, and that he thought they should go to Pitt County to try and find them. Will agreed it would be a good idea.

Next they discussed whether they should keep Laney and Aunt Celie in town for any potential court hearings, or if it would be wise for them to return to Beaufort and stay out of the stressful situation around Edenton.

Adam said he thought they should go back so that they could, among other things, let his mother and Emmanuel know what was happening and that it would still be quite a while before he returned.

Finally, it was decided that the four of them would leave in the periauger that Adam and his father had left in Edenton when they first went to Virginia. They just needed to get some supplies together first, mostly foodstuffs.

They would travel from Edenton across the Albemarle Sound, then down past Roanoke Island, through the Pamlico Sound, and then west on the Pamlico River, which would eventually become the Tar River as the body of water narrowed. According to Aunt Celie's description of where Annabelle's father's family lived, they would travel to a place called Salter's Ferry and then ask around to find out where his plantation was on the south side of the river.

Chapter Eighteen

IT WAS STILL AFTERNOON, AROUND three o'clock, when they left from the dock at Edenton en route to Salter's Ferry on the Tar River. They would have probably been able to make it to their destination much quicker if they mostly traveled overland, but Emmanuel's periauger had to get back to Beaufort somehow, so this just seemed to make the most sense.

Adam had traveled in that same vessel before with Laney and Aunt Celie. Martin had come with him that time. That particular occasion was Adam's first time traveling to New Bern and meeting Will and Catherine. Another time Adam and Martin had traveled with Aunt Celie from New Bern to Bath, and then back to Beaufort. That was around the time that Ed Willis was murdered.

They were all relieved that the weather was fair, only a bit cool, but definitely tolerable. It was much better than the rain and cold they had dealt with earlier in the week.

What a relief it was to Adam, since he knew the trip would be a long one—at a bare minimum, with perfect conditions, two days, but a more likely estimate would be three days, or even four.

It was as though Providence stretched out its hand and held off any adverse weather conditions, and instead kept the sun shining bright in the sky and the wind *almost* right so that they were able to complete the trip in just under three days. It did seem as though the wind was working against them for a short time, as they approached Bath, which was on the north side of the Pamlico. Adam suggested they dock in Bath Creek for a little while to refresh themselves.

Aunt Celie agreed and said as much. She mentioned that the Lord must've been looking out for them, because she had just been thinking of how much she'd like to get out and walk around on solid ground.

As they drew near to the creek, Aunt Celie told the same story to Laney and Will about her late husband, Old Charles, that she had told to Adam and Martin when they had come to this place a year ago.

"Lookathere, chil'ren." Aunt Celie pointed to a clearing of land along a high bluff on the western bank. "Y'all see that big ol' house right there?"

Will nodded.

Laney said, "Oh, that's lovely. I wonder how old it is."

"I don't rightly know that," said Aunt Celie, "but that right there's the first English house my husband ever went in. And that was the first time he ever set foot on Carolina soil."

"What is that place?" Will asked.

"You don't know?" Aunt Celie gave a little grin. She was picking on Will. He knew so much about everything else, Adam reckoned she was amused to be able to teach him a thing or two. She continued. "That there used to be the gov-na's house—a long, long time ago."

"That was the governor's house? Governor Tryon?" Laney said. "When was this?"

"Oh no, child, this was a long time before Govna Tryon. This was Govna Eden. And I think I done figured it was around seventeen and eighteen in the summertime when they brung my husband here. They was sixty Negroes they put out on the bank that day."

Adam smiled. He remembered hearing this story. "I asked her if they had a slave market, but that wasn't it, was it, Aunt Celie?"

Aunt Celie shook her head. "No, sir, it sure won't. They was brought here by that pirate Blackbeard."

"So that's how our grandfather ended up with Old Charles," Will mused. "I think I may actually remember hearing something about this when I was very small, but I haven't thought about it for ages."

Laney's eyes grew wide. "Well I never have! This is new to me."

"Does Charles Jr. know this is where his father first arrived in this colony?" Adam asked.

Aunt Celie shrugged. "You know, I really can't say. I don't know. I reckon he prob'ly do, but only if his daddy told him. I don't remember ever tellin him nothin about it."

"I see," Adam said. "I only asked because I wondered if he might've heard of any contacts here in this town."

Aunt Celie shrugged again and shook her head. "I wish I could tell you, but I just really don't know."

They came alongside the little town and docked.

"Maybe we could ask in town if anyone here has seen Charles Jr. and Annabelle," Will suggested.

Adam remembered the eccentric sheriff. "I think that's a good idea. In fact, there's a tavern up on the main street there." He pointed in the general direction, then looked at Aunt Celie. "You remember where it is, don't you, Aunt Celie?"

Aunt Celie nodded. "Yes, I do."

Adam said to Will, "How about y'all go there and see about getting something for us to eat? I imagine these women might like to see if they have any, uh, *accommodations* while we have this opportunity."

He knew better than to embarrass the ladies by looking at them after making that suggestion, but nevertheless he assumed they'd be grateful for the chance to use a proper *necessary* rather than having to squat on the riverbank.

"I'm going to go look for the sheriff," he said. "If it's the same man your cousin and I met last year, he seems like a halfway decent fellow. A bit odd, but if he hasn't seen Charles Jr. and Annabelle, at least I can let him know that if he hears tell of them in these parts to not believe what he might read in the papers."

"That sounds like a fine plan," Will said.

He and the women went up the hill towards the main street.

Adam made his way towards the gaol, which was a small cabin just a few dozen feet away from the Bath Town courthouse. Both of the buildings were, as Adam had observed on his previous visit to town, surprisingly small structures. Everything looked just as poor this year as it had the last. The courthouse and the gaol, as well as the pillory and stocks, were all still in terrible disrepair, although it did look like there was a new door on the gaol. Adam wondered what had prompted that improvement.

When he finally got up to the gaol, he noticed the door wasn't actually locked. He went over to the window and peeked inside, but it was empty. He suddenly remembered the town drunk, Bob Cobb, whom the sheriff had told them about last year. Evidently, Cobb was an indigent who played an old game with the local authorities by getting into some kind of mischief on particularly cold days so that he could spend the night in the town gaol, only to be let out again when they felt he'd served his time. Since the weather wasn't too bad right now, Adam assumed Cobb might be roaming around town, enjoying his freedom, but that he'd likely be right back in the gaol house if the temperature dropped.

He crossed the lawn over to the courthouse and went in. It so happened that the eccentric, old sheriff was just inside, sitting cross-legged on a bench along the back wall, reading a book.

"Hello there, Sheriff. Adam Fletcher. We met last year— around this same time, actually. Do you remember me?"

The sheriff lowered his head and looked over his spectacles before taking them off. He stood and said, "Hallo there, sir. I do indeed remember ye. Ye be the young fellow who cornered the villain Harmon Jones." He reached out and shook Adam's hand.

"You do remember. I'm glad to hear it," Adam said.

"Yes, of course. Your name has been well celebrated up here in this country, ye being a true hero and all of the rest." The sheriff beamed and genuinely looked proud to be face-to-face with Adam. Adam thought the whole situation was flattering but awkward. He certainly didn't feel like a hero. In the matter the sheriff was talking about, Adam had only wanted to get justice for the victims of a murderer, as well as keep the people he cared about safe. He didn't want to be rude, though, so he said to the sheriff, "That's very kind, sir."

He wanted to get right to the matter at hand, so he quickly changed the subject. "You must be wondering what brought me here today."

"Ah, do ye mean to say ye haven't just come to pay a visit?" The sheriff laughed at his own joke.

Adam chuckled along. "Well, actually I'm on my way to Salter's Ferry with some friends. I wanted to stop here, though, in case you might have some information that could help us. We're looking for two individuals, a man and woman, who have been wrongfully accused of being runaway slaves. Well, the man is accused of stealing the woman, but the fact is neither of them are slaves. The man was recently emancipated, and the woman was born free."

"And ye speak here of two Negroes?" the sheriff asked, scratching his chin, apparently in deep thought.

Adam quickly nodded in response. "Yes, yes! Have you seen them?"

The sheriff appeared to give the matter some thought, then said, "No. I tell ye true, I don't believe I have seen anyone like that. Would ye happen to know if they come by foot? Or boat? Or on the backs of horses?"

"I have no idea, sir, although I would guess on foot. As far as I know, they don't have horses, and I don't know how they would've come by boat."

"I'll tell ye what I'll do," said the sheriff. "I'll keep an eye open for stray Negroes roaming around. If I see 'em, I'll put 'em in the gaol for safekeeping. How about that?"

Adam shook his head. "They aren't fugitives, sir. They're my friends."

"But ye said they're runaway slaves."

"No, I said they were both free, but a man from up near Edenton named Sanger is claiming the woman, Annabelle, is his runaway slave and that the man, Charles Jr., has stolen or lured her away. I've heard he's put an announcement in the paper with rewards for their capture. I just wanted to tell you if you see them or hear about them, know that they *are not* runaways or thieves. They are both free Negroes, and they are in the employ of my good friend Will Martin, Esquire, of New Bern. He's here in town with me right now by the way, along with his sister, Laney, and their servant, Celie."

"Well," said the sheriff, "I'm not sure what ye would have me do. I'll certainly not be putting up two stray Negroes in the tavern. The gaol is the best I've got."

"Then probably the best thing for you to do if you see them is to let them go on about their business. Just know they are not criminals and any advertisement in the paper that says otherwise is fraudulent."

The sheriff furrowed his brow. "Hmm… I'll tell ye the truth, I'm not ordinarily in the business of looking the other way at something like that, but since I know ye to be a law-abiding young man, and the foil for the evil Harmon Jones, I will do ye this favor if I see these Negroes of which you speak. I will give them their leave to go their own way."

It didn't slip past Adam that the odd man seemed unable to acknowledge them as his friends but rather insisted on referring to them as "Negroes" over and over again. Nor would he acknowledge their freedom. It was as if to refer to them any other way would be some sort of blasphemy. Adam didn't bother arguing with the man about it but instead thanked him for at least not arresting them, and then he went towards the tavern to see if Will and the women were over there.

Sure enough, Laney and Aunt Celie were sitting on a bench out in front of the tavern, probably at Will's suggestion. Of course it also might've been that the tavern keeper didn't want a black woman in his restaurant, slave or free, unless she was working in the back.

It really was turning out to be an unseasonably lovely day. Not warm but not at all cold, and as long as it was in the sun, sitting outside was brisk and refreshing.

Adam explained to Laney and Aunt Celie what had happened with the sheriff. "At least if they pass through here, provided they haven't already, he'll know they're not runaways. He said he'd leave them alone. I'm hoping if he ever communicates with any other sheriffs or constables he'll pass the word along as well."

Aunt Celie didn't say anything, but she made her thoughts about the matter plain by folding her arms across her chest and uttering a simple, "Hmph."

It amused Adam a little bit that she reacted that way. She'd always been so incredibly reserved in his presence. One thing was becoming apparent on this particular journey, though. She was becoming more at ease around him. He almost felt like she was as comfortable and familiar with him now as he had observed her being with Laney and Will. And he was grateful for it.

Chapter Nineteen

WHEN ADAM AND COMPANY FINALLY arrived at Salter's Ferry, it was around seven o'clock. It was awfully late for them to try to find the plantation where Annabelle's father's family supposedly lived. Nevertheless, Adam and Will agreed that they should try. If Charles Jr. and Annabelle were somewhere in the area, they'd want to find them and let them know they didn't need to run any more.

Laney and Aunt Celie stayed behind in the boat while Adam and Will went to the plantation houses visible from the river. Fortunately, the second house they went to had a family living there who knew Annabelle's father's people—the Holmes family. After they were told where to go, Adam and Will went straight to that plantation. It was a little bit longer of a walk than Adam expected.

Will expressed what he was thinking: "I wonder if we should've left the women back in the boat. Do you think they're safe?"

Adam turned and looked back over his shoulder. "I think they should be fine. I can't even see them from here, but that means no one else can, either."

"Well, hopefully no one will come try to cause them any trouble."

Finally, they arrived at the landmark they were told to look for: two big barns side by side and a big two-story house with huge pecan trees out front.

"I'll do the talking," Will said.

That was fine with Adam. After all, Aunt Celie and Charles Jr. were part of the Martin family, and if anyone was going to help them get out of this situation— accused of being runaways and thieves—it would be Will. He was not only the former owner of Charles Jr. but also a well-connected lawyer.

The warm glow of lantern lights shining through the windows told them someone was home and unlikely to be sleeping. Will went up on the porch, and Adam followed close behind.

He pulled on the cord that rang the bell in the house. Soon a man who looked close in age to Will came to the front door.

"Good evening. Can I help you?"

He had only opened the door enough to stand there and speak to them. He certainly didn't look like he'd be inviting them in.

Will cleared his throat. "Good evening, sir. My name is William Martin, and this is my friend Adam Fletcher. We've come here because it's our understanding that this is the Holmes farm."

The man seemed a little confused at his visitors, but he nodded and said, "Yes, well it *was* the Holmes farm. It's the Williams farm now. I'm Jim Williams, and my wife, Betsy, was the daughter of Mr. Holmes."

"I see," said Will. "Well, the reason I've come here is

because I'm trying to locate a man and a woman who are missing. We have reason to believe they may have come here."

Jim looked skeptical. "I'm not sure why you'd think that. Who are these people?"

Adam and Will exchanged uncomfortable glances.

Adam wondered, *what if this man doesn't know his father-in-law conceived a mulatto daughter with one of his slaves?* Maybe they should've brought the women, after all, so they could ask to talk to the lady of the house without raising any red flags.

Will hesitated before giving a clever answer that avoided that particular issue altogether. "Specifically, we're looking for a Negro man named Charles and his wife, Annabelle. She's a light-skinned woman. Probably mulatto. Have you seen either of them?"

"There are no slaves on the Williams farm. I'm afraid we can't help you." Jim's reaction suggested that he was likely a man of antislavery sentiments, perhaps a Quaker.

Adam wanted to speak up.

"Well," said Will, looking in Adam's direction to ensure he didn't say a word, "Charles and Annabelle aren't slaves. They are both free, but they are currently on the run because a man north of here claims that Annabelle is his own runaway slave—which she is most assuredly not—and he has put out notices of rewards for their capture. We just want to find them before bounty hunters do."

Just then a woman heavily with child, whom Adam surmised was likely Betsy, formerly Holmes, the wife of Jim Williams, came to the door.

"Who are our visitors, Jim?" she asked.

"They're looking for two missing Negroes. I told them we haven't seen whoever it is they are talking about."

Adam could see a strong resemblance between the woman at the door and Annabelle. That would make sense if they were half sisters.

Jim seemed as if he was just about to send Will and Adam on their way when Adam felt he had to speak up.

"Are you Betsy?" he asked the woman.

The woman's eyes grew large. "How do you know my name?"

"Listen," Adam said, "there are two women waiting in a periauger down by the dock." He pointed north in the direction of the river. "One is Will's sister, Laney, and the other is a slave who has belonged to the Martin family for decades. They call her Aunt Celie."

Both Betsy and Jim looked confused.

Adam continued. "Aunt Celie told us there is a good chance that her son, Charles Jr., and his wife, Annabelle, had come here in search of safety."

Betsy looked stunned. "Annabelle?" She looked at her husband as though she were seeking his guidance on what she should say or do.

Jim shook his head and began to shut the door. "I'm sorry, we don't know anything about any Negroes."

Adam put his foot in the way to keep the door open. "Please wait. I promise you we are not here to take Annabelle or Charles Jr. away. We are their friends."

Will nodded. "Yes, they're part of our family. We're worried about them. Please, if they are here, just go tell them Will Martin and Adam Fletcher came looking for them, and see what they say."

Jim shook his head. He grabbed a flintlock pistol that had apparently been on a table near the entrance and pointed it at Will. "I told you, we don't know anything about these Negroes. Now get off my porch and leave my farm before I put a lead ball in each of you."

Both Adam and Will put their hands up and backed off of the porch.

"We're sorry to bother you, sir," said Will, "but if they are here, please tell them about us."

Adam and Will walked away from the Holmes farm at a brisk pace, frustrated about how the conversation with Jim and Betsy had taken place.

"I think they must have been there," said Adam.

"I agree," said Will. "But who knows if they still are? And regardless, if Jim Williams threatens to shoot anyone who comes after them, that will likely be a fair deterrent for bounty hunters."

"Sure," Adam said. "Except that reward is a lot of money, and it would only take one bounty hunter to put a lead ball in him before storming the farm and taking anyone who might be hiding there and God only knows what else."

Will nodded. They made it back to the periauger and were relieved to see that Laney and Aunt Celie were still there waiting, undisturbed.

"What happened?" Laney asked. "Did you find the Holmes farm?"

"Yes," said Will. "It's the Williams farm now, though, and Mr. Williams isn't very hospitable."

Aunt Celie looked worried. "My son won't there, then?"

Adam shook his head. "We don't know. If he is, I think

they're at least trying to protect him and Annabelle. He told us to leave or he'd shoot us, though."

Aunt Celie threw her hands up in the air. "Oh Lawd ha' mercy!"

"They might have already come here and gone," said Will. "Regardless, we don't need to make trouble with Jim Williams in case he intends to make good on his threat. The only thing we might be able to do at this point to call off the dogs is to go back to New Bern so I can get my paperwork regarding Charles Jr.'s emancipation."

Adam unfastened the lines from the dock so they could make their way back towards the Pamlico, but this time they all had to employ the oars to get the periauger going again, since the wind was not helping them.

They hadn't gotten more than a hundred yards from the dock when they heard a loud voice calling, though they couldn't make out what it was saying. Adam had everyone stop rowing so he could hear better.

"Mr. Will! Mr. Adam!"

He heard it that time. He held up his lantern to see if he could make out anyone in the distance, but it was useless. He shifted the tiller to get them headed back in the direction of the dock.

"Mr. Will! Mr. Adam! It's me, Charles Jr.!" the voice called out. "Come on back here."

"Good Lord!" Will exclaimed. "It's him! Thank God!"

"We're on our way," Adam called out in response. "We're on our way! Don't go anywhere!"

Soon they were back at the dock, and Charles Jr. was waiting for them there. He held his lantern forward so he could see to help them out of the boat. When he got close enough, he was able to see Aunt Celie.

"Mama! That you?"

"Yes, child. It's me! Help me get out of this thing." She held her hand up while he guided her out of the boat and onto the dock, followed by Laney, then Will, then Adam.

Charles Jr. embraced his mother and they sobbed in each other's arms.

"Jim Williams just got done running us off of that farm with a pistol," said Will. "We suspected you might be there, but I know better than to persist in trespassing where we aren't wanted."

"Is Annabelle with you?" Adam asked.

Charles Jr. nodded. "Yes, sir, Mr. Adam. We both came here when we 'scaped from the Sangers' place. I wanted to go to Beaufort, and we were on our way there, but it's so far and we was goin on foot."

"Have they been treating you both alright here?" Will asked.

Charles Jr. shrugged. "They ain't got no slaves, but they got some free Negroes workin here. I reckon they said they think slaveholdin's some kind of sin, but it ain't like they real friendly or nothin."

"Why are they letting you stay here, then?" Adam asked. He was skeptical of the circumstances.

"You ask me, Mr. Adam, I think it's just they's 'fraid of the scandal if folks see Annabelle roamin round here. She and Betsy Holmes—I mean Williams—sho 'nuff look like sisters."

Adam raised his eyebrows and nodded. "I understand how they might think that's a problem. I could sort of see that resemblance when we went up to the house."

"I heard just that," said Aunt Celie. "I heard that the old Mr. Holmes done marked his youngins good-fashioned. They *all* look just like he did."

"I can't wait to get a good look at this Betsy woman so I can see how much she and Annabelle favor," Laney said.

"So what do we do now?" Adam asked no one in particular.

"Do you think Jim Williams will tolerate us on his farm now that he knows you know us?" Will asked.

"Yes, sir," said Charles Jr. "Soon as y'all left he done told us y'all was here but that he sent you away. I told him why, then I come running after you. Y'all come on back with me and I think it'll be fine."

At that, all of them—Charles Jr., Aunt Celie, Laney, Will, and Adam—went back up to the Williams farm, and they were all welcomed inside by Jim and Betsy.

THINGS WERE EXACTLY AS CHARLES Jr. had described them. Jim Williams and his wife, Betsy, weren't unkind, but they also weren't especially warm towards Charles Jr. and Annabelle. It eventually became clear to Adam and the others that that the Williams' willingness to provide shelter to the couple was motivated primarily by two things.

First of all, Annabelle was worn completely out from the ordeal on the Sanger farm, and she desperately needed time to recover and heal from some of the injuries she had received while she was there and from traveling so far on foot from Edenton.

Adam and Will wanted to ask about what happened, but Charles Jr.'s change in demeanor when they began questioning her told them that this was a topic they should perhaps not persist in delving into. Betsy did acknowledge she was her half sister, and the fact that they favored so much made her feel some level of responsibility for her well-being.

Second, Jim and Betsy had said that Charles Jr. and Annabelle would need to wait and leave when the moon was closer to full. Right now the moon was waxing, but there was only a quarter, and it was cloudy. It would be several days before there was enough light for them to leave at night and still see where they were going. Traveling by day in this section of Pitt County was out of the question. Annabelle just looked too much like Betsy and her other siblings to be able to pass through the area without setting tongues wagging.

"I think we need to discuss what the law will require," said Will.

Betsy suggested that she, Annabelle, Laney, and Aunt Celie go into another room so the men could talk. They all got up and followed her out of the room.

Adam, Will, Charles Jr., and Jim Williams were all left sitting around the parlor. As soon as the women left, Jim Williams questioned Will about what he meant by "what the law will require."

"What I mean is that we have a complex situation here," Will said. "I'm already planning a suit against the Sangers for disrupting my business, as well as causing my property in New Bern to be left unattended against my wishes for an extended period of time due to their fraudulent claims that Annabelle is their runaway slave. One of the first things we'll do when we get to Edenton is insist that they bring their bill of sale for Annabelle to the court."

"There ain't no bill of sale for Annabelle," Charles Jr. argued.

"Exactly," said Will. "They'll likely bring whatever bill of sale they have for Peg, and then we'll use whatever details are there to prove Peg and Annabelle are not the same person. I'm also including in the damages that I'll be demanding they pay reimbursement for the travel expenses of myself, my sister, and Aunt Celie from Boston on *La Dama*, as well as my return transportation to Boston as soon as all of this has been cleared up. In other words, they have no idea of the trouble that they've gotten themselves into."

Charles Jr. raised his eyebrows. Adam could tell he was surprised that Will was actually going to go to this much effort to seek justice from the Sangers for what they had done.

Will continued. "Additionally, Charles Jr., you are fully within your rights to file your own suit against the Sangers for kidnapping your wife, as well as any lost wages the two of you might claim for being unable to work these last several weeks. I'm afraid you'd be unlikely to receive any compensation for the bodily and spiritual abuse that your wife has suffered, as well as yourself—and to be sure, no amount of money could make up for that, anyway—but I will gladly represent you, pro bono of course, in any matters in which we might actually have a chance of success."

Charles Jr. thought for a minute. "I don't know, sir. I don't know that I want to go back up there and have to see them people again. I mean, what they done to my wife and all…"

Adam could see that Charles Jr. was broken in spirit. He had no doubt that if given the chance, Charles Jr. would love to personally beat the living daylights out of Sanger and his right-hand man, Byrd. In fact, Adam wouldn't mind a chance at the two of them himself. But as things stood, he knew Charles Jr. knew he could never get away with seeking vengeance, and anyway, he was reminded of what his grandfather, Emmanuel, always said: "Vengeance is mine saith the Lord."

"I think you should take Will up on his offer," Adam said to Charles Jr. "As much as you can, within your legal limits, I think you should make those evil men pay. Set an example so that others might see that this isn't something that folks can just get away with."

"We won't have to get involved with any court business, will we?" asked Jim.

Will sighed before he answered. "We really don't need anything from you other than to please just help keep Annabelle safe while we handle everything."

"I'm not leaving her here," said Charles Jr.

"I don't blame him," said Adam.

Will responded, "Listen, Charles Jr., I understand where you're coming from." He then looked over at Adam. "And I don't blame him, either, Adam." He looked at both of them. "But we mustn't forget Charles Jr. is presently a fugitive. He's been accused of stealing a slave from the Sangers. Never mind the fact that she's not their slave, she's his wife, and she's never been a slave. Still, the accusation is there, and I'm afraid the attitude in Edenton is likely going to be that he's guilty unless we can prove he's innocent. And we can do that easily, but I'm afraid it's going to mean you *will* have to come with us back to Edenton, Charles Jr."

"Do what?" Charles Jr. asked. "Why would I have to go back there?"

"I'm afraid it's the way the law is handled. You've been accused of a crime. If you continue to run, you will appear guilty, regardless of your innocence. There are rewards out on you dead or alive. The only way to confront this is to come with me to Edenton. I'll testify to the fact that you were a slave belonging to my family until some months ago, but that I emancipated you through the proper channels in the Craven County court. I'll also testify to the fact that Anna- belle has been in the employ of my household for years now, and that I have always known her to be a free woman, and that there are countless individuals in New Bern who could testify to the same."

"What if they don't believe you?" Charles Jr. asked. "What if they's wantin to see Annabelle up at the courthouse?"

Adam could see the worry was consuming him.

"Well," said Will, "that's part of what my countersuit is about. I plan to bring so many complaints against them that they'll beg me to drop the cases. I have no intention of dropping everything, but I am certainly willing to drop some of the claims if it will cause them to drop their ridicu- lous accusations. Also, I will explain the circumstances of her health and injuries, and that it would have been inadvisable for her to travel back to Edenton. With the bill of sale—if they even have one—Dr. Bass can serve as an additional wit- ness that Annabelle's description does not match the one in that document."

"So, does that mean y'all are going to be clearing on out of here tomorrow?" asked Jim Williams.

"Actually," said Will, "I'm afraid we're going to have to rely on your hospitality a bit longer, if you don't mind. In fact, I'd like to leave all of the women here while Adam and I accompany Charles Jr. back to Edenton to take care of this business."

Jim didn't say anything right away. He wrinkled his brow and looked highly skeptical of the whole plan.

Finally, he spoke. "I think it might be better if all y'all just leave here tomorrow. Y'all came in a boat. Charles Jr. and Annabelle can leave in a boat without going through town. Maybe at least y'all can take them further on down the river back towards the sound. Won't that put them closer down to where they'd need to go, anyway, to go back to New Bern?"

Adam was growing increasingly irritated the more Jim spoke, and he said as much. "I thought y'all said Annabelle had injuries, and that she has suffered quite an ordeal at the Sangers' and on the arduous trip to this farm. Why in the world would you want to cast her out tomorrow when she can continue to stay here and rest and recover?"

"It's alright, Mr. Adam. I'd just as soon leave here, anyway," said Charles Jr.

"I don't doubt it," said Adam. "I'd probably feel the same way, but all the same, I think it's a sorry thing that they don't have the basic Christian compassion to want to provide shelter and care for a woman who is, by no fault of her own, a member of their family!"

"Now you're getting off into the weeds there, Mr. Fletcher," said Jim, pointing his finger at Adam. "We have Christian compassion or else we would've never opened the door to this pair in the first place. It's not as if Annabelle and Betsy grew up together. They'd only heard about each other through relatives. The fact is, we have to continue on living here once y'all are gone."

"What's that got to do with anything?" said Adam.

"I'll tell you what," said Jim. "Most of the folks who live around here really love their slaves. And I don't mean they *love* their slaves, I mean they love *having* slaves. And they have 'em out in the fields day in, day out no matter what the weather is like, working, working, working. I don't reckon y'all see much of that down around where you're from. Didn't you say you were from a port town?"

Adam nodded. "I'm glad we don't see a whole lot of that down in Beaufort. There are slaves, but they're not out working in fields."

"Huh!" Jim huffed. "That's just fine, but don't go thinking of yourselves as superior. Y'all just have different problems than we do. The fact is, we have no part of the slave trade. My parents were Quakers and I was born a Quaker, but I was dismissed for marrying out of unity. In other words, Betsy wasn't a Quaker, so they kicked me out of the church. Still, we don't believe in keeping slaves. Instead, we have several day laborers who we pay wages work for us, and it's already been a challenge to keep these two out of sight. Now you're wanting us to take on two more? A white woman *and* a black woman? And somehow we're supposed to keep them here for who knows how long? No, I just don't think we can do that. Too many questions. Too many problems."

Will sighed. "I'll admit I don't fully understand the circumstances here that would prevent you from continuing to provide shelter to the women, but by all means, if it's going to be too much trouble, how about if you just let me know where we could hire a coach, and I'll pay a driver to take them back to New Bern? Then we can carry on with our business in Edenton."

Adam thought Will making that suggestion was brilliant. The thing Jim wanted to avoid was letting anyone see this mixed-race woman, who looked almost just like his wife, but if Will was going to be forced to go into town to hire a coach to drive the women back to New Bern, far more people would see Annabelle and wonder what was going on.

Jim again took a moment before he spoke. He looked like he was contemplating something.

"Now let me just think about this for a minute…"

Adam, Will, and Charles Jr. all sat and gave Jim a moment to think.

"I've got a good-sized horse cart with a cover, and I've got a pair of good walking horses. If you're hiring a driver to take them to New Bern, why not just let me handle it?"

"That might work," said Will. "How much would you like me to pay you for it?"

"Just my expenses," said Jim. "I don't have a fancy coach, but I was thinking I could take them as far as Swift Creek. My aunt and uncle live over there, and he has a nice carriage that he could drive them in the rest of the way. The trip would be about thirty-five miles altogether, but them staying a night in Swift Creek would be a nice break in the journey."

"Alright, will it be just you taking them from here to Swift Creek?" Will asked.

Jim shook his head. "No, sir. I'll bring my wife. She's not so far along that it should be a danger for her to travel, but I'd feel better if she were with us, for propriety's sake."

"Very well, as long as you think she's willing to go."

"I think she'd be glad for the opportunity."

Chapter Twenty

WHILE CHARLES JR. SAID HIS tearful goodbyes to his wife and his mother, Adam was able to find a moment to speak to Laney in relative private.

"This has been quite an adventure this last week and a half, huh?"

Laney gave a nod. "It most certainly has."

"I wish we were all going back home now," he said.

"Me too." She smiled and lowered her head. She seemed nervous.

"We'll be back together again in Beaufort soon, though." He touched her hand, but only for a second. "It's been such a long time since we've both been home at the same time, hasn't it?"

She blushed. "It has been a long time. Months in fact."

"I suppose we'll have a lot of catching up to do when I finally make it back from Edenton."

"I'd like that," she said.

She started to turn and walk away but quickly turned back around and put her arms around Adam to give him a tight hug. He wrapped his arms around her to return her embrace, but no sooner had he done that, she took a step back and went over to climb into the wagon with Annabelle and Aunt Celie.

Adam waved goodbye to her.

ADAM, WILL, AND CHARLES JR. discussed the possibility of hiring their own coach to take them to Edenton, but it would've taken just as long, if not longer, to travel overland, and then there would still be the issue of getting Emmanuel's periauger back to Beaufort once everything was resolved. Before long, they were on their way, sailing east on the Tar River towards the Pamlico. It took them three days to make it back to Edenton.

They arrived at the town dock around ten o'clock in the morning on the third day. Upon their arrival, they went straightaway to Mr. King's place so they could determine what would need to be done to handle the matters at hand in court.

The three men were all thoroughly exhausted after what felt like days and weeks of endless travel. Nevertheless, it seemed the determination to see the events through to a successful conclusion gave them all the necessary strength to push ahead. They gathered with Mr. King in his office, where they mapped out their strategy for the coming days.

In response to hearing all of the plans, Adam asked the first question that came to his mind.

"What are they going to do to Charles Jr.? I mean, is the constable just going to take Will's word that he wasn't some accomplice to a slave attempting to run away? Or worse yet, that he outright stole her from the Sangers?"

"I'm afraid that the constable will likely want to hold

him in the gaol until both parties, or their representatives, can appear in court."

Surprisingly, Charles Jr. seemed to be much less anxious than Adam. Adam wasn't sure whether he had just resigned himself to fate, or if his faith was so strong that he believed everything would work out exactly as it should.

"Will he be safe there?" Adam asked.

Will looked like he wanted to answer the question, but he deferred to Mr. King.

"He should be. In fact, he'll definitely be safer in the gaol than he would be if he were still 'on the run,' as they might claim."

"Oh?" said Adam. "Are accused runaways and their abettors usually treated well here in Edenton? Because I've not heard of that being the case down our way."

Will seemed a little embarrassed at Adam's comments. "I'm quite certain that if the county knows that we have our eye on his situation, and that we're filing countersuits on his behalf, they'll treat him fairly. He'll hardly be their ordinary captured runaway."

"Huh." Adam rolled his eyes. "Well, thank God for that, then." He looked at Charles Jr. and said, "I reckon it's a good thing that you're not ordinary. I reckon having us white men on your side gives you a leg up. I'd hate to be the poor Negro without monied benefactors."

"Adam!" Will chastised him.

Adam knew he had probably gone too far with that last statement, but he was just so tired, which made it difficult for him to temper his speech. That, and it did grieve him to think of the fact that while Charles Jr. might receive mostly fair treatment because he had white folks intervening on his behalf, any other so-called runaway or Negro accomplice without such an advantage would most likely receive a strong dose of brutality and be thrown into slavery, even if they had been born free.

When they were done discussing all of that, Mr. King did offer to host Will and Adam at his house as soon as they finished up at the courthouse. They could wait there for a response from the Sangers. Will almost accepted the offer, but he apparently caught a glimpse of Adam's countenance, which made clear that was not a plan he favored. As a result, Will graciously declined and said they would probably be more comfortable taking a room at the tavern, as their schedules might be a bit erratic because of all the traveling they'd done lately.

The four men went to the courthouse. Mr. King introduced Will to the clerk of court, and then the two lawyers explained the circumstances and filed all paperwork necessary related to Will's complaints against the Sangers. Will then introduced Charles Jr. to the clerk and explained who he was and his history with the Martin family. He also explained about Charles Jr.'s wife, Annabelle, and how she had been born free and was so injured from mistreatment at the hands of the Sangers, as well as the arduous journey that she and her husband had undertaken to get away from her captors, that she was unable to make the trip back to Edenton to appear.

"Mr. Martin," the clerk said, "how am I to know that Charles Jr. isn't a slave? You're not known to this court, so I would have expected you to bring evidence to that fact."

Will's face fell. "I have his emancipation papers at home in New Bern. This situation is too urgent for me to have to travel back there just to bring you those papers. Even if he were a slave, I'm here on his behalf, so wouldn't you assume he belongs to me?"

Charles Jr. cleared his throat before whispering something to Will. Adam was able to hear him, though. "Um, Mr. Martin, sir. I have my papers."

Will's eyes opened wide. "You do? You mean you brought your copy?"

"Yes, sir."

"Well, that takes care of that, then," said Will. "Please show your paper to the man."

Charles Jr. took a folded-up piece of paper out of his pocket and showed it to the clerk. "See here? This paper says I'm free. I ain't nobody's slave."

The clerk looked through the spectacles that were perched on his nose and read the document.

"So it does."

The man seemed unsure of what to do with Charles Jr. given the circumstances. While he could now acknowledge the fact that Charles Jr. was a free man, he explained that they would still need to at least hold Charles Jr. until a subpoena could be delivered to the Sanger farm and for them to have the opportunity to respond one way or another.

THE CLERK ACCOMPANIED WILL, CHARLES Jr., and Adam to the gaol, which was a small building just a few dozen paces behind the courthouse. He had already sent someone to go fetch the constable to come open the gaol for their latest visitor.

Within a few minutes, a man who looked like he was around thirty or so, near Adam's height but with a bulkier frame, started walking towards the gaol.

"What've we got here?" he said as he approached the group of men.

"Constable Peck," said the clerk. "You already know Mr. King." He motioned to the newcomers. "This is Will Martin, Esquire of New Bern and a friend, Adam Fletcher."

"And who's this?" the constable said with a devilish grin while looking Charles Jr. up and down in a way that set off alarm bells in Adam's brain.

The clerk said, "You've heard about the complaint that the Sanger man made about his runaway slave wench."

Constable Peck nodded slowly, still grinning. "Yep... I do remember something about that."

"Well, this is Charles Jr., her husband. He's the man who was accused of taking her from the Sanger farm," the clerk explained.

"I see," said the constable.

"And of course the fact is that neither charge is true," said Will. "We've come to see to it that this whole matter is sorted out, but we've been advised that Charles Jr. will need to remain in the gaol until we've heard from the Sangers regarding our countersuits."

"Uh-huh," said the constable. He scratched at his chest while he continued to nod and look Charles Jr. up and down. Adam was getting increasingly agitated. He had certainly had his own experiences with corrupt and sadistic officials in positions of power, and he suspected Constable Peck might be another one of them.

"You reckon you're going to get this Negro out and take him home soon, then, is that right?" said the law man. "He won't be needing the hospitality of the good people of Edenton for too long, then, will he?"

"We certainly hope to sort this matter out so we can all go home soon," said Will. "Then we won't have to trouble you any further."

The constable stepped past the clerk and then over between Will and Adam before grabbing Charles Jr. by the shoulder of his shirt. "You come on, boy. Let's get you settled on in here so we can get this business taken care of."

Adam saw Charles Jr. tense up as the man grabbed him, but remarkably, he was compliant. Adam knew he wouldn't have likely have been so disciplined, and as a result, he'd have likely suffered an even worse punishment.

The constable roughly shoved Charles Jr. into the gaol and followed behind him. He then locked him in a cell. There were two cells in the building, but the other one was empty. It was definitely a fancier gaol than the one in Bath, which was only one large room with bars in the windows.

Will exchanged a worried look with Adam, but both men realized there was little they could do at this point except try to get the case before the justices as soon as possible.

The constable sauntered out of the gaol and then said to the others, "Don't you worry. We'll look after him."

Will held up a finger and said, "Constable, I'm sure you're very good at what you do. And I'm sure I don't need to remind you that this is an innocent man. He has done nothing wrong. This will all come out in the days ahead, but for now I'm confident that you *will* take good care of our friend."

Constable Peck smiled with one side of his mouth and wrinkled his eyebrows. "Oh sure, of course I will. Like I said, don't you worry."

Adam didn't know what came over him, but he suddenly

found himself opening his mouth to say something that he hadn't planned. "Uh, Constable, I'm sorry to bother you about this, but I was just wondering… Didn't I see you in a tavern up in Corapeake a few weeks ago?"

The constable twisted up his face. "No, I'm afraid you must have me confused for somebody else."

Adam bit on his thumbnail and looked pensive. He said, "Are you sure? I mean, the resemblance is uncanny… I could've sworn I saw *you* in the tavern at Corapeake with a whore sitting on your lap." He turned his attention to the clerk. "I'm telling you. I think this man may have been who I saw in Corapeake about three weeks ago. Does he have a wife? Does she know?"

The clerk looked shocked.

Will put his hand to his forehead, then quickly looked down. "Adam, I'm sure you're mistaking the constable for someone else." He looked at the constable. "Sir, he's been traveling almost nonstop for about a month now. He just needs a good rest."

Adam shook his head and stepped forward and got within just a few inches of the constable's face. "No—well, I mean, yes, I am tired, but I'd remember those ugly jowls anywhere."

He grabbed the constable's cheeks, which prompted the constable to quickly grab Adam's wrist and yank his arm downward. Adam used his other arm to shove back against the constable, nearly knocking him down.

"Adam! Good Lord!" Will exclaimed. "Have you lost your mind?"

The constable quickly got hold of both of Adam's arms and with the help of the clerk, forced him into the gaol. Adam put up a slight struggle, but not as much as he could have. They soon had him locked in the cell right next to Charles Jr.

"Don't worry!" Adam called out from the cell. "How can I tell your wife if I don't even know who she is? In fact, maybe the woman I saw *was* your wife!"

Adam could hear Will apologizing profusely to the constable as he, the constable, and the clerk left the gaol building and closed the door.

The truth was, Adam had most definitely *not* seen the constable in a tavern in Corapeake, and, in fact, he couldn't recall seeing any women of questionable virtue sitting on men's laps in his recent travels. He felt guilty about lying and he felt guilty about picking a fight, but something told him not to let Charles Jr. be alone in that gaol, and the only way he could think of staying close by was being thrown into a cell, himself. Maybe Charles Jr. would've been fine. Maybe nothing would've happened other than the constable's blustering, but at least this way Adam could keep an eye on things. It didn't take long after the others had walked away from the gaol building for Adam to begin to wonder what the punishment was for falsely accusing and attacking an officer of the law.

"What'd you do that for, Mr. Adam?" Charles Jr. asked.

Adam shrugged. "I didn't like the look of that constable. Just couldn't help myself."

Charles Jr. shook his head and chuckled. "I never took you for a brawler, sir."

"Eh... I've done some fighting in my day. That's how I ended up an apprentice. You know it was initially supposed to be a punishment?"

"Is that right?" Charles Jr. looked amused at that.

"Let's just hope and pray Will and Mr. King can get this whole mess sorted out soon."

"Yes, sir. We sure need to do that."

"Well, take heart," said Adam. "Right now I'm the only one in this gaol who has actually broken the law."

"I don't know how much of a comfort that is, sir. They might lash you for it."

Adam nodded and sighed. "I know."

ADAM AND CHARLES JR. TALKED a little bit after Will and the others had left, but sheer exhaustion eventually got the better of them. They both lay down in their cells and fell asleep.

After what had been apparently a few hours—evident by the change from day to night—Adam heard a noise outside on the courthouse lawn. He stood and realized the sound seemed like it was coming from behind the jail. He wanted to look out the window, but it was a bit higher than his head, even on the tips of his toes. He went over to the corner and grabbed the bucket that served as a chamber pot, and he turned it upside down. Fortunately, it was empty, although he wouldn't have gone so far as to call it clean.

He carefully stood on top of it, hoping it would hold his weight. If not, not only would his foot break through the bottom of the disgusting thing, but he'd also not have it to use in case he needed it.

Fortunately, it held out. He was able to look out on the lawn, though he wasn't able to see anyone. The moon was nearly full, so there was plenty of light in the sky. The main problem seemed to be that whoever it was had already come around to the side of the gaol—or at least they were no longer behind it. He turned his head to look out the window in the exterior wall of the cell that Charles Jr. was in, but he wasn't able to see anything. He could detect voices on that side of the building though.

"Who's out there?" Adam yelled.

The commotion woke Charles Jr. "What is it?"

"Someone's outside the gaol," said Adam.

When Charles Jr. saw Adam standing on the bucket, he turned the bucket in his own cell over and was about to stand on it.

Adam said, "No, wait." He stepped down off of his bucket and motioned for Charles Jr. to stay where he was.

"There's no telling who that is," Adam whispered. "You might not want to let them see you."

Charles Jr. stood against the wall just beneath the window and tried to listen to what was happening outside.

"You in there, boy?"

Adam knew that voice. He assumed that Charles Jr. would recognize it too.

It was Billy Byrd, the overseer from the Sanger farm.

Neither Adam nor Charles Jr. answered.

"I SAID, YOU IN THERE, BOY?"

The fact that he hollered made it no more likely that Adam or Charles Jr. would respond. No doubt he was looking for trouble.

Next thing Adam knew, a rock came flying through the bars of the window in the wall on Charles Jr.'s side of the gaol. It would've been more likely to hit Adam than Charles Jr. at that trajectory, but evidently Byrd didn't know that. In fact, he might not have even known Adam was there. He wondered if Byrd found out Charles Jr. was in the gaol because of the subpoena that was delivered to the farm that afternoon, or if Constable Peck had told him.

Adam and Charles Jr. exchanged exasperated glances. Adam took a deep breath and shook his head. Charles Jr. just sat with his back against the wall almost directly beneath the window.

Evidently, not responding was making Billy Byrd even angrier than he already was, because next he was banging a long stick back and forth along the bars on the window.

Finally, Adam had had enough.

"What's the matter with you, you swamp-dwelling hick? Go back to your hole and leave me alone! I'm trying to sleep in here!" He went over and sat against the north wall, which, though it was in view of the window from where the rock had come, was not directly across from it. He wondered if Billy Byrd might try to throw another rock from a different window, and he wanted to avoid getting hit if possible.

There was silence for a couple of minutes. Adam doubted that a mere insult sent the man running, but he did guess that Byrd was confounded to hear Adam respond rather than Charles Jr. and was perhaps trying to decide what to do next.

Next thing he knew, Billy Byrd's ugly face appeared up in the window directly above Charles Jr.'s head. He was holding a lantern. He was obviously standing on something. Charles Jr. pressed his body as much as possible against the wall.

Adam hoped that Byrd wouldn't be able to see anything straight down, since he couldn't put his head in past the bars. He squinted as he looked up into the light that Byrd was holding. It wasn't particularly bright, but his eyes hadn't adjusted to it yet. "Why are you here?" Adam said to him. "Can't you let a man sleep?"

"Who are you?" Billy Byrd asked.

Adam thought he must've forgotten his face since he had been out to the Sanger farm all those weeks ago, or maybe it was dark enough in the cell that he couldn't recognize him.

No, wait. Maybe it's the beard. He hadn't shaved since he'd been on this whole journey, so he surely looked different than he had that day.

"I SAID, WHO ARE YOU?"

Adam leaned back casually against the wall and kicked his legs out in front of him, crossing his feet. "I'm just a man trying to get some sleep, and now I'm going to have to contend with nightmares thanks to your ugly face."

"I'm 'on kill you, boy!"

Adam shook his head and laughed. "Somehow I doubt that. You're out there. I'm in here. Why don't you go run and tell the constable that you came and threw a rock in here at me and then you threatened to kill me because I said you were ugly? Because, you know when the constable comes to let me out in the morning with my lawyer, he's going to see this big ol' rock in the middle of my cell, and he's going to know I didn't go out roaming around tonight to get it. And now that I've seen your face, I'm going to tell my lawyer that you came and tried to attack me in my cell while I was sleeping. Then you'll be the one in here instead of me."

Actually, Adam wanted to pick up that rock and throw it directly at Byrd's face, and a few years ago that was likely what he would've done, but he knew better now. He had only ventured outside the law enough to get put in gaol with Charles Jr., but he sure wasn't interested in having to stay there any longer than necessary.

"WHERE'S THAT NEGRO, DAMNIT!?" Byrd raged.

"Why do you keep hollering?" Adam asked. "I'm right here. And I know it's dark in here, but I'd think you could see that I'm not a Negro." Adam looked around. "I don't see any Negroes in here. Do you?"

"I know he's here somewhere!" Byrd growled.

"Good! Go look for him!" Adam said. "Let me get back to sleep."

Byrd spat through the bars and then jumped down from whatever he was standing on. He hit the bars over the window with a stick one last time.

Adam finally looked over at Charles Jr. He hadn't glanced at him once since Billy Byrd started looking in the window. He didn't want to give away that anyone else was in the gaol.

Charles Jr.'s eyes were huge. He let out a great, big sigh.

Adam patted the air in front of him with his hand as if to say, *Just hold on a minute. Sit tight.*

After a couple of minutes had passed, Adam felt more at ease. He and Charles Jr. whispered about what had just happened.

"You think he could tell I was here?" Charles Jr. asked.

Adam shook his head. "No. I don't think so."

"He didn't recognize you, Mr. Adam. I thought he'd remember you from Sangers' porch that day."

"Me too. But I think it's the beard."

Charles Jr. nodded. "Oh, yessir… that makes sense."

"I don't think he'll be back tonight," said Adam.

"Me neither," Charles Jr. agreed.

They both lay back down in their cells and tried to get some sleep before the morning. Only now, Adam's heart was pounding too hard to sleep, so he did what his mother always used to tell him, and what had worked for him so many times in the past: he just prayed until he fell asleep. It didn't take long.

Chapter Twenty-one

A T DAYBREAK, ADAM WAS AWAKENED by the light streaming in the window on his side of the gaol. He felt like he'd had a ton of bricks dropped on him. Having a tired body and sleeping on a hard floor were not conducive to a restful night's sleep.

Once he was able to convince himself to move, he shifted over and looked at his pocket watch for the time. He wondered when someone would come back to the gaol to check on him and Charles Jr. He slowly sat up and then stood reached his arms out in front of him to give his back a good stretch.

"You get any sleep, Mr. Adam?" Charles Jr. asked.

"Oh, you're already awake," Adam said. "How long have you been up?"

Charles Jr. shrugged. "Don't know. I don't think I really slep' much last night, anyway."

"I wonder how it works in gaol," Adam said. "I mean, do they feed us on some schedule, or just whenever they think about it?"

"You hungry?"

"Yeah, I'm hungry," said Adam. "We haven't eaten anything since yesterday afternoon. You're not hungry?"

Charles Jr. shook his head. "No, sir. I don't think I could eat anything right now."

"You got Annabelle on your mind."

"Mmm-hmm."

"She's fine now," Adam said. He sat against the wall nearest to Charles Jr.'s cell. "She's not at the Sanger place anymore. And we'll get you back to her soon."

"They gon' leave us alone, though? Or is they gon' keep botherin us even if we get out of here? Like that man did last night."

"I don't think he counted on things going the way they did last night. That rock is still there in the middle of the floor, right where it landed. I imagine Will is going to be here sometime soon, and he'll be able to see that with his own eyes, and maybe he can add another complaint to his case against the Sangers. Enough things on the list and I reckon they're going to back off for sure. Sanger isn't going to want to lose his farm, but he'll know that's a possibility if Will is successful with the charges he's making—and he should be successful, because they're all true. I don't think we'll have to worry about keeping that Billy Byrd in line. I reckon Harold Sanger will handle that himself."

"I sure hope you're right," Charles Jr. said.

Two hours passed before anyone came to the gaol to check on them, but Adam was relieved to see it was Will and Mr. King. They'd come with the constable, who was to release the two immediately.

Will explained to Adam that they were almost done, but

there was one last thing to take care of before they'd be able to go home.

"Wait? So everything with the Sangers? Annabelle? That's all resolved?" Adam asked.

Will nodded. "Dr. Bass's testimony that Annabelle would've had no scar on her face had it not been for the recent one meant that she couldn't have been the Sanger's runaway, Peg. That, along with my own insistence that Annabelle and Charles Jr. have been in my employ for so long made it a rather easy win, I think."

Charles Jr. clasped his hands in front of him and bowed his head. He looked like he was praying.

"You don't look happy, though," Adam said to Will. "There's something wrong, isn't there?"

"Come with me," Will said. Adam and Charles Jr. followed him.

As they walked in through the back door of the courthouse, Will told Adam, "Charles Jr. is free to go, but you assaulted Constable Peck yesterday. The magistrate wants to see you. I've already discussed your case with him, but he wants to decide on your punishment now. The only thing I can advise, Adam, is that you answer him truthfully and *be respectful*. This is no time for one of your outbursts."

Adam grimaced. It would've been just too straightforward if they had been able to leave Edenton so easily after all they had been through.

Mr. King told him that he was sorry there was nothing more they'd be able to do in his circumstances. He bade them all farewell as Adam, Will, and Charles Jr. entered the chambers.

After what seemed like lightning-fast questioning by the

magistrate—Constable Peck standing by with a smug look on his face the whole time—and Adam answering everything truthfully and as respectfully as possible, the magistrate took a moment and looked at both men, then sighed.

"I've heard the circumstances here, and while I do understand the motivation behind your actions yesterday, Mr. Fletcher, I'm afraid that we have laws and they must be followed—otherwise, we have chaos. That said, you will have to pay a penalty for your assault on Constable Peck yesterday."

Adam hardly thought of it as assault. He squeezed his face, shoved him, he was rude to him, but it wasn't like he punched him or anything. Which made the magistrate's next words even more shocking.

"I order that Mr. Adam Fletcher receive nine lashes well laid on his bare back, at which point he will be free to go. Case dismissed."

At that, Constable Peck motioned for another man to follow them outside of the courthouse. He led them out in the middle of the courtyard to the whipping post, where two other men motioned for Will and Charles Jr. to stand in a particular area.

The officer of the court who would be meting out the lashes came forward and ordered Adam to remove his shirt. Adam couldn't believe everything was happening so fast, and for what he thought was such a minor offense.

He removed his coat, his waistcoat, and his shirt, and then he was led over to the whipping post, where his hands were bound with leather straps.

The officer then walked a few paces away with the whip.

Adam stiffened his back and braced himself.

The officer drew his arm back and then...

Whack!

The sting of the whip caused Adam to arch his back…

Whack!

Now he was bracing himself for another hit…

                                        Whack!

                    Whack!

Whack!

                        Whack!

        Whack!

                                    Whack!

Whack!

Adam had been in many fights over the years, and his mother had certainly whipped him with a switch many times as a boy, but the sting of that whip ripping across his back and his sides made those experiences seem like child's play. He would never forget what had just been done to him, but he still didn't regret getting thrown into that jail cell with Charles Jr. If he hadn't and Charles Jr. had been left there alone, there was no telling what might have happened. In fact, he realized he should be grateful he only received nine lashes when the usual punishment was usually thirty-nine. The magistrate had shown him mercy.

He knew that the lashing most likely had nothing to do with shoving Constable Peck but was rather done at the constable's insistence, backed by the county court, so that he pay for humiliating him for the benefit of helping a Negro, even though that hadn't been the official charge.

Will later explained to him that the punishment would've been much greater, but the magistrate had, in fact, decided to be merciful on account of Adam's age and on the agreement that Will, Adam, and Charles Jr. would leave the county as soon as possible.

Chapter Twenty-two

ADAM, CHARLES JR., AND WILL went straight to New Bern upon leaving Edenton, as that was where the women were. It took them two and a half days, so that put them arriving at the town docks at around nine o'clock at night.

Will was able to quickly hire a coach to take them to his house, a trip that wouldn't have been a long walk, but the three were just far too exhausted.

They hadn't carried much with them to Edenton from Salter's Ferry—the women had gone back to New Bern with most of that—so there was no luggage to unpack. Will said they should go to the front door so as not to startle the women inside by coming in the back. Candles were aglow in the windows, so he assumed they were awake.

He gave the door a sturdy knock.

Laney came to the door, and her face immediately broke into a huge smile. She was such a beautiful sight to Adam, her honey-colored hair illuminated by the light of the candlestick she was carrying. She stepped back so the three weary travelers could come inside, and then the men took off their coats and hats.

When Adam turned around, Laney must've caught sight of the blood on the back of his shirt because she gasped and put her hand on his shoulder above the many stains and said, "What's this?"

"I'll leave you to explain that to my sister," Will said to Adam. "I'm nearly sleeping on my feet, so I'm going upstairs to get out of these disgusting clothes and I'm going to bed."

Apparently, he hadn't even given a thought to the impropriety of leaving his sister alone downstairs with Adam. Perhaps the events that had transpired in recent weeks made the usual social expectations seem somehow less important.

Charles Jr. was visibly anxious to see his wife, whom Laney told him was back in his cottage with Aunt Celie. He went straight through the house and out the back to see his family.

That left Adam and Laney standing alone together in the foyer.

She stood facing him and took a deep breath.

"We're an ugly sight, aren't we?" Adam joked.

Laney shook her head. She reached up and wrapped her arms around his neck and held him tightly. "Oh, thank God you're here! I have been so worried about you. All of you!"

Adam dropped the small bundle he had been carrying and put his arms around her as well, and he breathed in deeply. Her hair had the faint scent of roses. He couldn't help but wonder if she always smelled like that, or if she was wearing rose water.

"I've thought so much about you," he whispered in her ear.

"And I you. What have they done to you?" she asked.

He could tell her voice was quivering, like she was about to start weeping. "It's a very, very, *very* long story," he said.

They held each other's embrace for a moment longer. When Adam's lips lightly brushed against the top her her ear she gave him a final squeeze, then stepped back and smiled and grabbed his hand. "Tonight you should rest. Tomorrow you tell me all about it, alright?"

"You probably don't even want to know."

"I want to know everything about you," she said with a smile. Then she leaned forward and gave him a small kiss on his cheek.

Just then Adam and Laney were both startled to hear, "Uh-huh, I thought so. I know how you chil'ren are." It was Aunt Celie standing in the doorway of the foyer. "I reckon it's time you go on up to bed, girl. Don't you?"

Laney smiled once more and gave Adam's hand a squeeze before going up the stairs to one of the guest rooms.

Aunt Celie told Adam she'd come in from the back of the house to give her son and his wife some privacy. Truthfully, Adam was grateful for the interruption. He wasn't sure that he was quite ready to have that talk with Laney yet—the one his father had suggested he have—and he also wasn't sure that given his level of exhaustion, both physical and emotional, he could maintain any sense of decorum with this young woman he so deeply loved.

"Mr. Adam," said Aunt Celie.

"Won't you please just call me Adam, Aunt Celie?"

The woman let out a big sigh and shook her head. "Mr. Adam, I just heard about what you done for my son."

Adam couldn't respond. He didn't know what to say. He just smiled.

"I just wanted to tell you thank you, and I 'preciate you always being so kind and decent to me and my family."

"Well," said Adam, "of course, Aunt Celie. You're part of the Martin family—a family that I hope you know I love deeply—so if you, or Charles Jr., or Annabelle, or the grand-babies they're bound to give you one day ever are in need of help, you can think of me as family too."

At that, Adam and Aunt Celie said good night, and soon the whole house was sleeping.

Acknowledgements

As ALWAYS, I THANK GOD FIRST, for allowing me to continue writing and publishing, and for blessing me with such supportive and loyal readers. I WANT TO ACKNOWLEDGE MY SON for being my in-house consultant for character and story development. I love bouncing around ideas with him and hearing his perspective on Adam's circumstances and choices. And since he is a fellow creative, and a young man only a few years younger than Adam's character, I value his input and ideas for unique ways to tackle tricky plot points. TO MY BROTHER SAM, THANK YOU for helping me think through all of my obscure questions related to colonial North Carolina laws. I'm so happy you're my brother and that you're as brilliant as you are, because I'm fairly certain I couldn't afford your legal consulting fees if I had to hire you! Finally, I want to say thank you to nautical history and ship-rigging expert, Courtney Andersen

— aka "the man who helped Capt. Jack Sparrow look cool" — for graciously allowing me to tap into his wealth of knowledge and experience with a many months-long stream of questions about ships and sailing. *The Stolen Bride* is even better than I could have expected thanks to his input. (READERS: *Check out my fascinating interview with Mr. Andersen, where he discusses his work designing the ships and rigging for the* PIRATES OF THE CARIBBEAN *films, as well as how he got interested in ships and sailing in the first place. He also mentions some of his favorite things about the Adam Fletcher series*: http://bit.ly/AndersenQA)

—S.D.G.—

*The next few pages are a sneak
preview of the forthcoming...*

CHRISTMAS
IN
BEAUFORT

Chapter One

THE MILD NOVEMBER DAYS THAT the residents of New Bern were enjoying lately provided a welcome time of rest for Adam Fletcher and the companions of his most recent series of journeys. They had taken him from Beaufort to Boston with a number of unexpected, and highly stressful, stops along the way.

He knew his family would be worrying about him back in Beaufort. He also couldn't help but wonder how his father had fared on his own leg of the journey. After dropping Adam and Will off in Edenton, Santiago had gone much farther south — towards Havana — with a number of his crew-turned-mutineers being held on board his sloop, *La Dama*.

If it weren't for the absolute exhaustion that was felt by Adam and the others after their recent ordeal, along with the fresh scars on Adam's back from the lashes he had recently received, they would have likely already left for Beaufort with Laney and Aunt Celie.

As it was, however, Dr. Beasley, a kind-hearted old physician, was checking in each day to look after Adam's wounds.

He recommended that Adam stay put for at least a few days to give his injuries a chance to scab over well and that he not risk possibly being caught in rain or other circumstances that could interfere with the healing.

That first morning after the night Adam, Will, and Charles Jr. had arrived back in New Bern, Adam was taken by surprise after breakfast when Laney and Aunt Celie insisted he remove his shirt and lie down on the settee in the parlor so they could examine his wounds, and clean and dress them.

Dr. Beasley arrived as they were finishing up. When he saw what they had done, he commended the women on doing a fine job of cleaning the lash marks. "It'll make my job a good bit easier," he said.

Adam was still stretched out on his belly, his head resting on his arms. He tried his best to see what the doctor was doing.

"Laney, why don't you take that out back so Dr. Beasley will have room to work," Will suggested. He was referring to the basin that Laney and Aunt Celie had used for cleaning Adam's wounds. It was still on the table next to the settee.

She nodded and took the basin and rags out of the room.

The old man sat in a chair that had been pulled right beside the settee and opened up his medical bag. It contained a number of small bottles of a variety of tinctures that Adam couldn't begin to identify. However, he ended up taking out was a jar of a substance that *did* look familiar to Adam.

"Is that honey?" he asked.

"Mm-hm," Dr. Beasley replied, as he took some cloth strips out of his bag and draped the bundle in a pile at the small of Adam's back — the only area of flesh that was not covered in angry red stripes.

The doctor turned and looked at Aunt Celie. "I forgot to bring a spoon. Go get a spoon for me, please."

Aunt Celie gave him a nod and said, "Yessir," and then went into the dining room to find a spoon. She brought it back to him, and then she excused herself to tend to other work.

Dr. Beasley plunked the spoon down into the jar and began applying honey directly to the wounds on Adam's back. He only spread it on the areas where the skin was visibly broken. There were some welts where one could see that he had been struck, but the skin was intact. The doctor wouldn't worry about those, but across the the broad, muscular part of Adam's back and his shoulders, there were several places that had been torn by the whip, and they looked like they were beginning to show signs of infection.

"Are you just going to leave it like that?" Adam asked, as he felt the sticky substance getting slathered onto his skin. It did burn a little bit — but then again, anything touching those cuts would've burned.

"I'll be covering the honey with these bandages. The honey is sticky, of course, so the bandages should stay in place. Do you have a clean shirt?"

"Hmm..." Adam wasn't sure what to say. He looked over at Will, who was standing by the door that led to the foyer.

Of course he didn't have a clean shirt. When he began his travels a month ago, he didn't expect to be gone longer than overnight. He definitely didn't bring many changes of clothes.

Will said, "I have something clean he can wear."

"Well," said Dr. Beasley as he applied the last bandage, "you'll want to put on a clean shirt to keep all of this covered."

Adam nodded. "Alright."

"Try to keep everything dry," said the doctor. "I suppose after a day or two we'll know if it's time to remove them. We'll have to wait and see how they're healing up."

The doctor put the jar of honey and a couple of leftover bandages back in his bag and then he stood from his chair. "Well, I suppose we're finished here," he said. "I'll come back to check on you tomorrow."

Adam rose from the settee. He shook the doctor's hand and thanked him for coming by and tending to him.

The old physician excused himself and left.

Adam felt a bit awkward, standing there while he waited with a back full of uncomfortable sticky bandages. He glanced across the room and noticed Laney standing near the door to the hallway. When his eyes met hers, she blushed and said, "Oh, I was just looking for Will."

Just then, Aunt Celie called to her from somewhere down the hall. "Your brother's done gone upstairs to fetch a shirt for Mr. Adam," she said.

"Oh? Good! Thank you," she called back in response. "I'll go find him, then." She smiled at Adam and then disappeared down the hall, heading towards the stairs.

Adam suspected the girl wasn't looking for her brother, but he figured she was clever for trying that excuse, anyway. He was also amused that Aunt Celie was evidently watching her like a hawk.

One thing was certain: Things had definitely changed between him and Laney now. He wondered how things would be once they were all back in Beaufort.

He remembered what his father and Martin had said to him about letting her know of his intentions, but he still didn't think there was any need to do that anytime soon. What would be the point?

And speaking of Martin, he wondered what had happened with him and Jenny Green... and Hardy's brothers.

Well, one thing was certain, there would be plenty of catching up to do when they all got back home.

To be continued...

SIGN UP FOR
THE GAZETTE
FOR BOOK UPDATES AND
SPECIAL DISCOUNTS.

Go to AdamFletcherSeries.com/subscribe

Have you read all of Adam Fletcher's Adventures?

Book 1

THE SMUGGLER'S GAMBIT

Book 2

CAPTURED IN THE CARIBBEAN

Book 3

MURDER IN THE MARSH

Book 4

THE GYPSY'S CURSE

Book 5

THE STOLEN BRIDE

More titles are forthcoming.

Subscribe to THE GAZETTE *newsletter at*
AdamFletcherSeries.com/subscribe *for updates.*

www.ingramcontent.com/pod-product-compliance
Lightning Source LLC
Chambersburg PA
CBHW022108240626
47153CB00007B/2278